ADVISING THE VISCOUNT

ANNABELLE ANDERS

IN FOR A PENNY PUBLISHING, LLC

Advising The Viscount

Copyright 2022 by In For A Penny Publishing, LLC and Annabelle Anders

Cover by Barbara Cantor, Forever After Romance Designs.

✺ Created with Vellum

SO MUCH FOR BACK-UP PLANS

- The Scandal that never was
- One room, one bed
- All thanks to a blunder in the London Gazette.

Jilted and scorned, Miss Adelaide Royal has lost any hope of landing a proper English husband thanks to her industrialist American father's disdain for nobility. Lucky for Addy, teaching at Miss Primm's provided her with the perfect "back-up plan."

London's golden lord, Damien Reddington, the Viscount Bloodstone, is determined to recover the legacy of his father's estate despite his humiliating secret. He will brew and sell the best ale in all of England and if he fails to turn a profit, he has a "back-up plan." He's not only handsome, but titled, and if necessary, Damien will fill his coffers by marrying well.

Or so he thinks.

Acting as witnesses at a secret wedding, Addy and Damien land in the most unlikely of scandals, forcing them to temporarily pretend to be man and wife as they flee London.

Will this unlikely couple miss the silver-lining in this cloud of chaos, or will they hand over their hearts and never look back?

\

INFATUATION

"Do you take this woman to be your wife?" The question echoed off the towering stone walls around the empty sanctuary.

Miss Adelaide Royal held her breath as she waited for the groom's response. Not *her* groom. Never *her* groom.

"I do." Captain Sterling Edgeworth answered.

"He'd better," Addy mumbled to herself and relaxed her grip on the flowers she held for the bride—one of her dearest friends, Miss Chloe Fortune—soon to be Mrs. Sterling Edgeworth.

Chloe answered thusly to the same question and Addy sent a half-smile across to the only other witness present—Viscount Bloodstone—who caught and held her gaze with a solemn nod.

As per usual, staring into his unusually-colored eyes, of course, reduced her legs to the consistency of pudding. Although firmly on the shelf, she wasn't immune to appreciating such a fine specimen of manhood. Sometimes, in fact, she found it nearly impossible to look away.

. . .

HIS FACE WAS elegant without taking anything from his masculine appeal. The effect of his broad shoulders, sharp cheekbones and commanding jawline sent a shiver through her. The beauty of his violet eyes and full upper lip turned that shiver into a warm caress.

He was the sort of man to inspire romantic poetry.

He was the sort of man to sneak into her dreams.

This morning, the viscount wore an impeccable gray morning suit and not only outshone the groom, but the bride as well.

It was a travesty for one man to be so beautiful, but Addy wasn't about to complain.

"Let us bow our heads in prayer," the priest commanded.

She forced herself to focus on the bouquet Chloe had shoved back at her before the ceremony began. It featured daisies but also dill, herbs, lavender, and sage. Addy was rather proud of the collection she'd assembled for her friend and only wished Chloe was taking the wedding more seriously.

Unable to stop herself, she cast another furtive sideways glance from beneath her lashes. Lord Bloodstone's feet were planted shoulder-width apart with his hands clasped behind his back. He ought to look relaxed in such a stance, but he appeared distinctly alert.

AND THEN HE LEANED FORWARD, catching her watching him. Even in the dim light of the church, his magnificent eyes sparkled. When he winked, Addy's knees nearly gave out completely.

Her secret infatuation was getting out of hand. She was in a house *of God*, for goodness' sake.

She refused to entertain even one more fanciful thought, squeezed her thighs together, and forced herself to pray.

"Dear lord, I ask that you bless Chloe and Captain Edgeworth's marriage so that it is fruitful and happy. Soften my father's heart to relinquish some of my funds. And please help Allison Meadowbrook see the error of her ways..." And last but not least... *"But also please, please, keep me from saying anything stupid in front of the viscount..."*

She forced her breaths to come evenly.

"Amen," the viscount's voice boomed over the others.

Sunlight slanted through the windows, and as though painted by the hand of God, Lord Bloodstone's streaky blond hair transformed into spun gold.

He possessed a feline quality that reminded her of one of the paintings she'd seen in the museum—Daniel in the Lion's Den. His pupils gazed out at the world lazily from beneath hooded eyes and his indigo irises glowed with mysterious intensity, reminding her of a lion.

She shivered.

Only when Captain Edgeworth turned with Chloe on his arm at the conclusion of the ceremony, did the Viscount actually smile—a little lopsided but unselfconscious.

The fact that his smile wasn't perfect made him...

Even more perfect.

The four lone participants then followed the priest across the altar to the table where the license waited to be signed. Chloe and the captain went first and then the priest slid it across the surface to Lord Bloodstone.

The viscount lifted the quill and stared at the document

with a puzzled expression. And of course, Addy watched him.

Something was not quite right, though. What was he waiting for?

Standing beside the viscount, the hairs on the back of her neck stood up.

He was bent over and seemed to be studying the document.

Was he waiting for the priest's signature to dry? Was he reading the fine print to assure everything was on the up and up? But no…

He squinted down at the paper, seemingly perplexed by the official, artistically drawn words explaining the purpose of the certificate. Did he have something in his eye?

He'd dipped the quill into the small jar of ink but then paused with his hand hovering over the paper.

"Right here," Addy pointed to one of the lower lines. The ink clung perilously to the tip of the pen, seconds from dripping onto the parchment.

She didn't want Chloe's marriage certificate to be marred by a careless blob of ink.

"I'm quite aware." Lord Bloodstone glanced over his shoulder and scowled. "Thank you." He then turned back and painstakingly formed the letters of his name. Once finished, he presented the quill for her use with an exaggerated bow. "It's all yours, Miss Royal," he smirked.

Never in her presence had Lord Bloodstone behaved with anything but consideration and charm. Had she prodded at a weakness or…?

She'd been wrong to assume he'd been perplexed. Of course, she was wrong. Heat seeped up her neck and then spread into her cheeks. "I meant no offence."

"Why would I be offended?" He raised one brow.

Perhaps he'd had something lodged in his eye after all. Or perhaps he normally required spectacles.

It was possible, even, that he'd become emotional and teared up at the conclusion of the ceremony.

But...

As Addy met his clear stare, she did not really believe any of those possible excuses.

When he'd caught her watching him, his countenance had turned defensive—similar to when one of her students struggled with a difficult problem or assignment.

His frown had been one of frustration. Embarrassment. *Fear.*

"Of course. My apologies, my lord." Addy tried to dismiss her suspicions and signed her own name just below the viscount's, forming elegant curls and loops.

Likely, this would be the only marriage certificate she'd ever have the opportunity to sign so she would make darn certain her signature was neat and tidy.

The viscount's troubles had nothing to do with her or the ceremony or the certificate—best she minded her own business.

Addy had her own affairs to attend to before leaving London, and now that this wedding was finalized, she would go to the one place in London that ought to have been like a home. The memory of her aunt's all-too-quiet townhouse brought familiar emptiness.

With the ceremony concluded, the priest crossed his arms and waited patiently while the four of them lingered at the altar.

"My congratulations," Lord Bloodstone shook Edge-worth's hand.

"I appreciate you standing up with me," the groom responded. "And my thanks for ensuring Miss Royal returns safely to the school..." Captain Edgeworth's gaze flicked in Addy's direction, followed by the viscount's amused one.

"But of course," he said.

Addy frowned and turned to convey her opinion of the exchange to Chloe. She didn't require a keeper. She was perfectly capable of travelling without a protector.

Her friend merely grimaced with a shrug.

Addy sighed.

She would not argue with the newly married couple just now. As they all stepped down from the altar, she edged away instead to make herself invisible.

This moment was for Chloe. It was for Captain Edgeworth.

This moment represented the end of one era but also the beginning of another.

Chloe was married.

Priscilla was married.

Victoria was married.

And now that Addy had completed her task as companion and chaperone, she would track down her father before traveling back to the all-girls' school where she taught—Miss Primm's Private Seminary for the Education of Ladies.

Chloe, now Mrs. Sterling Edgeworth, was the fourth teacher to marry since Addy had begun teaching at Miss Primm's. The autumn session was only six weeks away and would bring not only the return of their students, but at least two new teachers.

Addy dropped her gaze to the bouquet Chloe had handed off and refused to take back. Carrying flowers felt awkward—as though she, and not Chloe, was the bride today.

Perhaps the servants at Victoria's townhouse, where she was residing for the duration of her visit, would appreciate them.

Despite lacking ribbons and lace, and guests, and fancy gowns, the ceremony had been a romantic one. Candles burning on the altar cast long shadows on the ceiling and crumbling stone walls, and there was a certain charm to the mismatched chairs sitting empty in the vestibule.

Addy shivered.

"Even in summer, these old buildings stay cold, don't they?" The viscount appeared at her side, all affability once again as he slid his arms out of his jacket. "Take this."

"That's not necessary—" Addy shook her head. The instant they stepped back onto the London street, the heat of summer would press in around her again.

And yet, as he settled the jacket on her shoulders, Addy burrowed into it gratefully, inhaling and identifying leather, soap, mint and... a uniquely masculine spice.

Before the ceremony had commenced, Captain Edgeworth had informed Addy that he intended on taking Chloe to his family's Mayfair townhouse directly afterward.

The two of them would wish to be alone—that's what newly married couples did. The priest went about extinguishing candles while the bride and groom strolled toward the exit leaving Addy alone with Lord Bloodstone.

Soon enough, she'd be truly alone.

Not that she was incapable, but she could hardly remember the last time she'd been allowed a few days of solitude.

Back at the school, her colleagues, her students, their

parents, and of course Miss Primm kept her well-occupied. Faced with only one responsibility in town, she felt oddly disconcerted.

But also, uniquely free.

Was this what it felt like to be a man? She glanced over at Lord Bloodstone, who stared curiously at the bouquet.

"She didn't want it." Addy flicked her gaze to the offending bouquet. She was not the one who'd just been married. She wasn't even close. "I thought Chloe would want any luck she could get, and that it could make the ceremony a little more romantic…"

"But this wedding wasn't meant to be romantic, was it?" Lord Bloodstone made a scoffing sound but winged an elbow in her direction. She felt unusually small and vulnerable with her hand tucked in his arm.

Unfortunately, he was right.

The ceremony hadn't been planned or wanted by either party. No, Captain Edgeworth and Chloe—Mrs. Edgeworth now—had genuinely trapped one another into it.

Addy sighed. "They may not have married under ideal circumstances but I am hopeful they find happiness together…"

She felt foolish for the romantic suggestion as he drew her away from the church.

"We're more likely to find a hackney this way," he said as he led her across the road. "Shall we?"

Addy had to tip her head back to see his expression and blinked, feeling almost blindsided by the perfection of his elegant profile. His mouth stretched into a practiced smile and his gaze held hers for the perfect amount of time.

Addy wasn't fool enough to read anything other than kindness into his charm. He'd do the same for any lady standing alone at the conclusion of a private ceremony such as this.

"Thank you." Addy would accept his assistance in hailing a hackney so that Chloe and Edgeworth could drive away unconcerned.

Following their departure, Addy and the viscount could go their separate ways, each to attend to their own business.

But Lord Bloodstone, it seemed, had other ideas.

"I'll see you safely to your friend's townhouse. My apologies for not providing a private carriage, but a hackney ought to be along shortly."

Surely he didn't mean to escort her back to the townhouse.

Alone.

"And as soon as you're ready to return to the country, I'll accompany you back to Miss Primm's."

NOT THE NEWLYWEDS

*D*amien steered Miss Royal around a steaming mess in the road. Absent his assistance, no doubt, she'd step right in it.

The woman seemed lost in her own thoughts most of the time. And when she didn't have that faraway look in her eyes, she was the opposite—noting far too much for her own good.

What would it be like to know Miss Adelaide Royal's thoughts?

Not that he'd ever have the chance.

...Or that he'd want to.

The church bells chose that moment to begin ringing, and a few passersby shot them curious glances.

"Felicitations to you," a fruit vendor called out and Damien startled. *Felicitations for what?*

The man's stare shifted to the woman at his side and understanding struck. Carrying the traditional bouquet of flowers, she appeared more bridelike than the actual bride had.

No doubt, casual observers might believe himself and Miss Royal to be the newly married couple. Damien chuckled.

Those observers could not be more wrong.

No, when Damien married, his bride would not be some schoolteacher, but a proper lady, hand-picked to suit his needs.

Damien shot his gaze to the woman beside him. Strawberry-blond curls dangled around her face and neck to rest at the edge of her bodice, and unwittingly, he flicked a glance at her generous bosom.

And just as quickly forced himself to look away.

In all the handful of times she'd been foisted on him, he had, in fact, exchanged less than a dozen or so words with her. Now, having promised Edgeworth he'd see her safely back to Miss Primm's, he supposed he was going to have to remedy that.

She was American, something he'd be able to decipher by her mannerisms even if he hadn't heard her speak.

But aside from the natural assumptions one made about schoolteachers, he knew very little about her.

Most women who traveled from the colonies came to England intending to land a husband, and yet this one had taken employment. If she came from any sort of money at all, she'd have been already scooped up by one of the poverty-stricken lords that hung about Mayfair.

She glanced up, her emerald eyes veiled by thick lashes, and blushed.

Standing beside him in her straw bonnet holding a collection of yellow daisies and other fragrant greenery, she looked quite countrified.

"I'm sorry." She glanced around and then shrugged. "The attention. It's the flowers."

He afforded them a quick glance. "But they are pretty."

"I arranged them myself," she said. "I've added herbs to the blossoms to ward off bad spirits."

Good lord... "Are you a superstitious person, Miss Royal?"

"Not really." She shrugged again, her frail shoulders brushing his arm. "Did you know that the Greeks and Romans wore wreaths and carried bouquets as symbols of new beginnings? And of course, also of fertility."

Miss Royal rarely met his stare and upon mentioning fertility, she dipped her chin even lower.

The marriage they'd witnessed had already been blessed in that particular regard... or would be before the end of the year.

"In ancient England," she continued, almost sounding British but for the relaxed cadence. "People believed that a bride represented good luck. But, of course, you know this already." She ducked, biting her lip.

"Do go on, I'm fascinated."

She tilted her head, staring at him with a narrowed gaze, but then went on to answer his question. "In order to capture some good luck for themselves, people chased after brides, tearing off pieces of their clothing, ribbons, sometimes even their hair. To protect themselves, brides began carrying bouquets. That way, when attacked by a mob, she could toss the bouquet in one direction and escape by running in another. So the tradition was rather practical, in its own way."

"Since the bride refused this particular bouquet, does it

hold good luck?" Good luck, he presumed, was lady-speak for 'finding a husband.'

"That remains to be seen." She glanced down the street, behind and then forward. Even more onlookers now noticed and followed. No doubt, they weren't interested in the bouquet so much as they hoped he'd be tossing them coin.

And judging by her pinched mouth, the encroaching crowd made her more than a little nervous.

Sounds of a horse approaching presented a quick escape, however, and Damien raised his hand and hailed the hackney as it turned the corner.

"You mustn't concern yourself with me after today, my lord." She smiled bravely. "Coachman John will see me safely back to the school."

Damien was not about to leave this woman to her own devices.

As the hackney drew to a halt, Miss Royal slipped out of the jacket he'd loaned her, and then, shrugging whimsically, threw the bouquet into the gathering throng.

The women let out a weak cheer and without thinking, Damien reached into his pocket and tossed a handful of coin.

He climbed into the vehicle behind her, shaking his head at himself.

"You've made their day." She blushed, not meeting his gaze.

He'd offended her earlier, after she'd noticed his hesitation signing that damned marriage license. How was anyone expected to read when the words were written with more loops and curls than a debutante's coiffure?

"So not all you bluestockings are opposed to marriage."

Disapproval of the institution was a common opinion held by Miss Primm's teachers. Most notably—and ironically—the new Mrs. Edgeworth.

"It can benefit both partners," she conceded. "If two people love and respect one another, that is. And as long as they value the other person for their character rather than what they have, or what they look like..."

"So you believe in fantasies."

"Perhaps," she sighed beside him.

Damien would not have expected this woman to be a romantic. Not because she was unattractive, but because, unlike most ladies of his acquaintance, she showed no desire whatsoever to... attract.

With a little effort, the auburn hair falling out of her coiffure promised to be luxurious. And if she would wear clothing that complemented her lush figure rather than hid it, more than one gentleman might set his cap for her.

But not him.

With instructions as to their destination, the hackney driver turned his horses away from the densely populated neighborhood.

"When would you like to leave London to return to Miss Primm's?" He couldn't linger in London too long.

His meeting the previous day with the three brewers from Stoke on Trent—Misters Greer, Millner and Carlisle —had been encouraging. He'd managed to negotiate a working relationship with the established businessmen.

They produced mostly porter and he would sell a weaker ale. With the Beer Act having given a rise to stiffer competition, it behooved all of them to join forces and garner more of the market.

They all stood to gain by pooling their resources. Damien was confident in his decision.

Having invested a good portion of his coffers into what had once been his father's expensive hobby, Damien was damned if his efforts would fail to turn a profit.

He needed to return to Reddington Park, improve on his strategies, and tweak his primary recipe while also ensuring the tanks were being properly cleaned before they could begin a new batch.

He also needed to meet with other distributors. Businessmen who stood to benefit from selling a less expensive blend—men who would be his allies.

But before he could do any of that, he had promised to accompany Miss Royal back where she belonged, safely ensconced at Miss Primm's with at least a dozen other spinsters and her classroom of budding debutantes.

Miss Royal, unfortunately, failed to share his urgency. "Not tomorrow." She stared at him with a frown. "I have... business to attend to first." She smoothed her gown. "I realize Captain Edgeworth and Chloe asked you to escort me back to the school, but I assure you it isn't necessary. Coachman John is quite capable."

"Oh, but it is necessary, Miss Royal." His word was only as good as his actions. "The day after then?"

The hackney driver drew them to a halt outside of a typical Mayfair townhouse not far from the park. Not allowing Miss Royal any opportunity to argue, Damien climbed out and then assisted her down to the pavement.

Did she not realize how delicate and vulnerable she was?

Staring up at him with the sun shining on her face, the vibrant green of her eyes was almost startling. She blinked and Damien noticed that although her long hair was a blondish red, her lashes were several shades darker.

"But it isn't entirely proper, is it?"

She was not wrong.

Escorting the spinster without another lady to chaperone conveyed a certain amount of social risk. He and Edgeworth had discussed the dangers on the highway, however, and considered her safety more important than propriety.

"I'll ride outside. And if we run into any acquaintances, we'll simply pretend you're my American cousin."

He could almost read her thoughts as she weighed his suggestion.

"Very well." She dipped that little chin of hers. "I have some errands I must complete first but I'll try to be ready by the middle of the week."

With that settled, Damien took her hand and bowed over it. She wasn't entirely comfortable with the gesture, and her cheeks never failed to turn pink when he made it.

It was, indeed, a shame that she wasn't dowered.

DEAR AUNT GEORGIA

The following morning, Addy stared up at a more familiar, but less welcoming townhouse a short walk from the one she'd been residing at.

Seven years had passed since she'd lived in her aunt's townhouse—where she had made her come-out shortly after her father brought her to England.

Where everything she'd ever believed about herself had changed forever.

"When should I collect you?" Coachman John asked from behind her.

"You needn't. My aunt's driver will convey me home." It was possible she'd have to walk. Trouble was, she had no idea how long this meeting was going to take.

Primm's loyal driver frowned in disapproval but climbed back onto his box.

"I'll wait until you're inside."

She had been more than willing to walk to her aunt's townhouse, but the driver had insisted upon conveying her, gently reminding her that they weren't in Warstone Crossing. "*In Mayfair,*" he'd said, "It is not appropriate for a lady to stroll the streets alone."

In Mayfair, Addy thought, it was not appropriate for a lady to do much of anything alone.

Addy shook her head with a rueful smile, trying to be grateful. It was ironic, though, that her employer's driver cared more for her well-being than her own father.

Ironic but nothing new.

Years had passed since she'd last seen him—since he'd bothered to show his face.

She pressed her fist against her chest as though she could rub out the empty ache there. In all that time, however, it never went completely away.

Would it ever?

The true nature of his feelings would be known soon enough. Because ultimately, where her father was concerned, his caring wouldn't be conveyed with words, or even with his attention.

But with money.

And until she addressed this issue with her dowry, she'd never know.

As a young girl, at home in the small town she'd grown up in, she'd been recognized and respected as the daughter of the very powerful gold mine tycoon, Mr. Charles Royal. It hadn't mattered if she wore the wrong color bonnet, or didn't sit straight enough. Everyone from the milner's wife to the governor's daughter had recognized her. She'd been quite pleased with her life in general, and if not for a meddling letter from England, she could have gone right on living in such contentment.

Three days after her sixteenth birthday her father had received a letter from her mother's sister, Aunt Georgia, reminding him of the promise he'd made at Addy's mother's funeral that he'd allow his daughter to debut in London when she came of age. And although he'd resisted for two years, her father had eventually given into his aunt's haranguing.

Shaking off those memories, Addy straightened her shoulders just as the door to her aunt's townhouse opened.

When some of her confidence fled.

"May I help you, Madam?" He was not the same butler she'd known years before.

If not for the familiar antiques displayed behind him, Addy would worry that she had the wrong residence.

"Yes. Er... I am Miss Adelaide Royal, here to visit my aunt, Miss Georgia DeClair."

Her chest squeezed, but then a recognizable silhouette appeared at the top of the elegant staircase.

"Adelaide Elizabeth!" Aunt Georgia lifted the hem of her skirt and descended. "This is certainly a surprise. Morris, take my niece's coat." She nodded at her servant and then turned back to scrutinize Addy. "You look even more like your mother than you did before. Although dearest Lizzy was so very refined before she ran off with your father. She must have been near your age when she passed. In my memory, however, she'll forever be the diamond of the season, that sweet girl of ten and seven. How old are you, now dear? Eight and twenty?"

"Seven and twenty," Addy turned her cheek to receive her aunt's formal kiss and swallowed hard. Addy's mother had willingly given up her place amongst London's elite to marry her father and move to America. Unfortunately, she'd died of consumption at the age of four and twenty, shortly after Addy turned six.

She'd left Addy with memories that felt more like dreams—of a sweet and loving mother—of tender hugs and ultimate safety.

Although her Aunt Georgia resembled Addy's mother in a physical sense, the similarities ended there.

"And what, pray tell, brings you to London, Adelaide?" Aunt Georgia turned to her butler. "Have tea sent up to the drawing room."

Addy's aunt would not want her servants listening into her conversations. She had always been very careful to avoid gossip.

Obviously, her aunt hadn't changed in that regard.

It was her primary reasoning for sending Addy away, of course.

Addy entered her aunt's favorite room. "You've changed it." Eight years ago, the furniture and décor had been done up in forest greens. Everything now consisted of soft mauves.

"One mustn't allow details to fall to the wayside, not if one wishes to hold court, so to speak." And then her aunt's expression fell. "But I know you didn't come here to discuss my furnishings."

Addy didn't have to guess at her aunt's concern. Eight years before, Addy's broken engagement had nearly cost Aunt Georgia her place in society.

"I want to find my father," Addy would not prevaricate. "I *need* to find my father. Do you know where he is staying?" Addy held her breath. Her father could very well be on the opposite side of the world. "I need to speak with him."

Aunt Georgia wrinkled her nose as though catching wind of a bad smell. "Why would you ever want to speak with that blighter—after what he did to us? It's incomprehensible."

Addy folded her hands in her lap. "Because he is my father." She had been prepared to meet with resistance and had a plan. "I need to discuss funds with him."

"I'm hoping you don't mean to bring up the subject of a dowry again. Your father said he'd never pay one and you know as well as I that once he has his mind set, he doesn't change it—stubborn fool that he is." Her aunt leaned forward. "You aren't entertaining a proposal, are you?"

The last time a gentleman had been interested in Addy, her prospective groom had been sorely disappointed.

As had Addy.

In fact, by the time the engagement ended, all of society shunned not only Addy but also her aunt.

"No," Addy quickly calmed her aunt's fears.

They'd shunned her father as well, of course, but he didn't concern himself with such trivialities.

"I want to sponsor some charity students." Addy used the story she'd decided on earlier. It was partially true, after all. But Miss Primm's financial circumstances weren't Addy's to divulge. "And I ought to have access to some percentage of my funds." Which had originally belonged to her mother.

At this, her aunt looked relieved and then thoughtful. "That's very charitable of you." Her aunt would embrace anything so long as her niece didn't come to her with expectations.

Although her aunt felt some responsibility for Addy, it was no secret that she wasn't eager to bring her into her home again.

For that very reason, although Addy corresponded with

her aunt on a regular basis, she wasn't welcome—even for holidays.

And the notion of sponsoring charity students wasn't completely false. Addy was willing to do whatever worked to bolster the school's finances. "It isn't fair he keeps all of it. I'm a grown woman and have a right to access at least some of what ought to have been my dowry."

Her aunt stared at her looking sympathetic, summoning a flash of memory that might have been of her mother.

She could never be quite sure.

"He's been back from India for some time now. It's my understanding he's conducting business down at the docks." She held up a hand. "He hasn't made his usual visit yet, but I've been expecting he would soon." Because, as her aunt had kept her informed, he made it a point to check on Addy.

In his own way, her father cared about her. It was just that he cared so much more about his business.

After they'd arrived in England together he'd seemingly handed her care over to Aunt Georgia. And he'd done so without shame, stating that ladies needed ladies to guide them. As a man, he was in no way equipped to launch her into adulthood.

"He still asks after me?" Addy asked.

"It's the only reason he comes."

He wasn't the most nurturing of parents, but he was her father.

Her aunt brushed a stray strand of bright red hair away from her face. "It's doubtful he'll hand over any funds. Why would he do that?"

"Perhaps if I suggest it as an investment." Business was the only language her father spoke. If her father agreed, Addy could always go to Miss Primm and ask about becoming a silent partner. Although Miss Primm could be independent to a fault, Addy had no doubt the school director would entertain such a proposal if things were as dire as Addy suspected.

Aunt Georgia frowned at Addy. "You're asking to be disappointed."

She might be at that. But perhaps her father had softened. And Addy wanted to be of help. If she could, she'd like to take some of the worry from the woman who was more than an employer.

Her father didn't need the money. It would be far better spent on the school than sitting in a bank somewhere.

"You needn't put yourself out like that," Aunt Georgia continued.

"I know."

"I would provide the funds myself, but you know my income is limited." Aunt Georgia explained. Again, this came as no surprise to Addy.

Because Georgia DuClair maintained her lifestyle, not because she invested well, but because of penny-pinching habits.

"I know Aunt, I know," Addy reached out a hand. "But will you send him word that I need to speak with him? Please?" Her hands shook at the possibility of seeing her father again after all these years—despite everything he'd done.

Because of what he'd done.

Her aunt pinched her mouth together. "There's no guarantee he'll even come…" She glanced around the room, as though fearful of how this could disrupt her comfortable life yet again.

Addy persisted.

"But you will send him the message? I can't remain in London for more than a few days. I need to get back to the school." Addy handed across a paper with directions to Victoria's townhouse that she'd written out earlier. "This is where I'm staying."

"If you insist." Aunt Georgia dipped her chin, looking relieved no doubt, that Addy wasn't going to ask to stay with her. "It's not as though it'll make much difference. There will always be more charity students than there are funds."

Addy had forgotten how negative her aunt could be and was glad she'd never need depend on her again. It was best this way.

Even so, when her aunt escorted her back into the foyer, Addy leaned across to embrace her. This woman was her last known blood relation.

But that too, was a mistake.

Aunt Georgia stepped backward causing Addy to falter. And it shouldn't hurt, but... it did.

"Well then." Addy stared everywhere but her aunt. "You will send word to him?"

"Of course. I said I would, didn't I?"

Addy rolled her lips together, nodding.

Her aunt had never been an affectionate woman and Addy did her best not to take the rejection personally.

She reminded herself that not all English people were so aloof. Miss Primm wasn't, nor was Chloe, or Victoria, or Priscilla.

Although Beatrice, the composition and literature teacher kept her distance.

Those in the *Ton* lived lives based on other priorities— status and money. And since Addy lacked the first, she'd been regarded for the second—one hundred thousand pounds worth.

When her father had taken her dowry out of the equation, her so-called friends had magically disappeared. And since her aunt couldn't disappear, she'd found a way to send Addy away.

Addy stepped outside onto the walk and refused to look back.

LORD BLOODSTONE'S PROMISE

*M*ayfair sat empty most of the summer months with good reason. It was insufferable.

Damien swiped his brow and lengthened his strides, cutting through the park on his way to the townhouse where Miss Royal resided.

Temperatures in London were ridiculously hot this time of year and he looked forward to returning north, to his estate near the sea.

Hopefully, she'd have completed her business and would be prepared to depart tomorrow morning.

It was possible her urgent appointments were nothing more than a little sightseeing. Not that he begrudged her a little sightseeing, but perhaps he could convince her to put it off until another visit.

He turned to step onto the walk and had to throw his hands out when a force of rose-colored muslin nearly ploughed him right over.

And when the woman driving that force tipped her head back to apologize, he found himself gazing into familiar green eyes.

Eyes that burned with a tumult of emotions.

"Miss Royal!" He gripped her shoulders, steadying her. Was she shaking?

"Lord Bloodstone! I'm so sorry. Did I hurt you?" she apologized, brushing at her skirts and looking flustered. "I wasn't watching where I was walking. I suppose I imagined myself the only person foolish enough to come out in this heat."

Damien glanced around. "You shouldn't be, you know—walking around Mayfair alone, that is." But that only garnered him a frown. "I was just on my way to Lady Rosewood's townhouse."

She grimaced, obviously grasping the reason for his visit immediately. "I'm not ready to return to the school just yet." She lifted her chin. "You mustn't allow me to keep you from going on your way. I have Coachman John, you know."

But her cheeks were flushed and her eyes a little too bright. Damien released her shoulders and stepped back. She was obviously upset about something.

He wasn't about to abandon her here alone.

"I'm not in that much of a hurry." Not so much that he'd break a promise. But what must he do to move matters along?

He gestured toward a path that would take them meandering through some giant oaks. And as he guided them both into the shade, he asked, "How can I help you? There must be something I can do to assist you with these tasks you must accomplish before returning."

She stared down at the ground. "You mustn't concern yourself, my lord." Not so much as a breeze stirred the atmosphere, and yet her voice fluttered on the air around him. "No doubt you have concerns of your own."

"What could possibly trump the worries of a lady such as yourself?" Damien might not be the smartest gentleman in the ton, but he knew women.

This one, he realized, was not going anywhere until she'd accomplished whatever it was she'd set out to do.

But he must be patient. Rather than press for details, Damien walked silently at her side.

"I'm not a lady." Her response wasn't at all what he expected. "I'm a schoolteacher."

"I would argue you aren't limited to one or the other."

She shot him an admonishing glance. "You needn't, but... thank you."

"You're welcome." Damien shook his head. Unwilling to argue the point, he returned to the matter at hand. "Now, are you going to tell me what's troubling you or are we to converse about the weather instead?"

When she didn't answer, Damien added, "Come now, we're friends, are we not?"

Another of her disbelieving glances. "Are we?"

"Of course we are. Now," Damien said, "Out with it."

This time she exhaled a loud breath.

"It's complicated," she began, and then sighed again. "On days like this I wish I'd never left America."

"Is it London in particular that's turned you off, or the English in general?" he teased gently.

"Please, don't be offended, but... a little of both?" A row of pearly white teeth came out to bite down on her bottom lip and Damien lost his train of thought.

"Pardon?" He flicked his attention back to her eyes.

"Present company excepted, of course."

"Of course." Damien nodded. "But it's natural, isn't it, to be homesick?" Without waiting for her to answer, he asked, "How long since you left America?"

"Nine years! Can you imagine?" Damien steered her around a root that protruded onto the path. "Sometimes America feels like another lifetime, and other times it feels like I left yesterday."

"Do you have family in England?"

"Hm…" She pondered a question that he considered straightforward. "My mother died when I was a child and my father…" she exhaled. "Well, I never know quite where he is. I have an aunt in Mayfair—my mother's sister. I'm just coming from seeing her, in fact."

Now they were getting somewhere.

"And after seeing her, you feel troubled. Is she unwell?"

"Aunt Georgia?" Miss Royal's head turned in surprise, and then she snorted. "Oh, no. She is as hearty as they come."

"And yet you were so distracted from your visit that you nearly ran me over."

"As a gentleman, I'd think you'd not mention that."

"Ah, yes. The collision was entirely my fault. Damien conceded, nudging her gently with his elbow. "Is that better?"

A hint of a smile curved her mouth. "I suppose."

The trees rustled and a teasing breeze languished in the air. Damien relaxed his shoulders, appreciating any respite from the heat.

Or was it her smile that set him at ease?

29

"Was I imagining your distress?" Damien kept his question light, not sure why he would press her on this.

Not everyone appreciated discussing personal matters and he wasn't about to force his assistance on her.

"If you must know," she finally broke the silence that had fallen between them. "I'm trying to locate my father, and my aunt wasn't at all encouraging." She exhaled a long, burdened sigh. "You saw the damage at the school before coming to London."

Damien and Edgeworth had indeed traveled to Miss Primm's to collect the captain's bride. When they'd arrived there, they'd learned that some scoundrel had set fire to the third floor of the school while the staff had been away on holiday.

"I did." With the plans for his brewery taking up most of his thoughts, Damien had all but forgotten. "The Marquess of Sexton is heading up an investigation. If anyone can get to the bottom of it, he will."

"Yes, well. Even so, repairs cost money." She frowned. "I fear Miss Primm might be in need of funds and I'm hoping my father will be able to help." She hesitated. "I trust you're aware of the necessity for discretion, I shouldn't even tell you, really... Anyhow, I cannot return to the school until I've found him." She turned to pin her gaze on him. "Therefore, I release you from your promise to escort me home."

"That's considerate of you, however, you cannot release me from a promise I made to someone else." Damien pointed out.

But her objective gave him pause. Who was her father that she'd turn to him for funds? And she was correct in that discretion was imperative. If word got out that the school was facing difficulties, parents would begin pulling their students left and right.

English society was particular in that, rather than rally around and help shore up such an institution, they were the first to abandon the endeavor at the first sign of weakness.

One never wished to associate with a sinking ship— socially or financially.

A TALK WITH A GENTLEMAN

*I*f it had been spring, if the season had been in full swing, a spinster walking with such a handsome and elegant viscount would have been remarkable indeed.

Addy could hardly believe it herself.

Even so, the very few visitors to the park cast curious glances in their direction.

Following the debacle of her failed engagement, the last thing Addy ever sought or wished for was to be noticed and did her best to ignore the stares.

Likely, it was the viscount's looks that drew most of them anyhow. He ran his fingers under his cravat, causing his shoulders to strain against the fabric of his jacket. What would he look like without his jacket?

Addy pulled her fan out of her pelisse and waved it before her face.

And yet the viscount seemed totally unaware of the attention. He was handsome, honorable, thoughtful, *and modest*—a potent combination.

It was the middle two characteristics that no doubt had motivated him to walk with her today.

"I don't know when I'll hear from my father." She pressed her point. Hopefully, Aunt Georgia would keep her promise. Addy ducked her head. "So please don't delay your journey home on my account."

Chloe and Captain Edgeworth should not have asked the viscount to provide her with protection. Addy didn't require a keeper. She was a grown woman, for heaven's sake.

Furthermore, she hated being a burden to anyone.

Lord Bloodstone halted and raised his free hand to his jaw. "What do you plan on doing until your father contacts you?"

The question surprised Addy.

"I... I don't know. I hadn't thought that far ahead." She supposed she'd do a lot of reading.

"Well, if we're going to wait, we might as well entertain ourselves, don't you think?"

"You mustn't worry about me. Coachman John—"

"Doesn't get paid enough to keep tabs on you." The viscount shook his head.

"Whereas you do?" Addy countered.

"Whereas, whether you like it or not, until I deposit you back at the school, you're my responsibility."

He wore such a charming smile, spoke in such a cajoling voice, that it took a moment before his words made sense.

"I'm not a child!" She frowned. "I'm no one's responsibility but my own."

"Of course you aren't." The viscount turned them along the path again. "But you could be a wise old octogenarian and I'd feel the same."

"If I was a wise old octogenarian, I highly doubt I'd be in this situation." Or perhaps she would—so long as her father controlled her funds.

"True. But I'd still be responsible for you," he pointed out with a teasing smile. "Have you visited Gunter's? Or the menagerie? I suppose you'd like to take a day to walk along Bond Street."

Addy barely contained the urge to stomp her foot on the ground. How could he be so overbearingly insufferable and charming at the same time?

"Lady Rosewood's library will keep me occupied. Where should I send word when I'm ready to leave?"

"My townhouse isn't far from here. Coachman John knows the way. Have you eaten yet today? I've yet to stop in at my favorite pastry shop." Was he truly so oblivious to her protests?

"You mustn't concern yourself with feeding me—"

"They have the best chocolate truffles in all of England." Addy nearly stumbled when he mentioned one of her greatest weaknesses.

Dash it all. He wasn't playing fair.

She licked her lips. She'd not had a bite of chocolate since arriving in Mayfair.

"I suppose that would be… nice," she answered. She'd allow herself this single indulgence. But only once, and only today.

And then she would firmly send him on his way.

"Splendid." They'd emerged from the trees and he led her out onto an open field. "We'll cut across here. It's not far."

Along the way, they strolled past three other couples and

a trio of giggling ladies, all of whom did nothing to contain their curiosity. Addy frowned.

If she were to take him up on his offer to escort her around London, she'd have to endure stares like this over and over again.

She'd rather sit in the library reading alone.

After she enjoyed a few chocolates, that was.

And yet, despite her reluctance to give into his chivalry, Addy found that walking and talking with Lord Bloodstone was entertaining in and of itself.

He was not self-involved as he easily could be. He was not oblivious to her as a person.

"What subjects do you teach?" he asked as they fell into a more purposeful pace.

"Math and science."

"Did you select those subjects or did Miss Primm suggest them for you?" No one had cared about these sorts of details before.

"I'm knowledgeable enough, and it was the only open position at the time," she admitted. "But I enjoy teaching them. And I like that there is always something new to learn."

"Do your students like you?" His smirk ought to have been annoying and yet oddly enough, it wasn't.

"My answer to that might change depending on the day of the week." She grew thoughtful. "Did you enjoy school?"

It was his turn to frown.

"I'm more of a hands-on person, so at the risk of disappointing you, I'll have to say mostly no."

She'd taught long enough to know that not everyone was suited for school. But that didn't mean they lacked intelligence or ambition.

Take her father, for instance. Addy shot the viscount a sideways glance. She couldn't pinpoint it exactly, but Lord Bloodstone seemed to possess a few similar qualities that reminded her of him. A focus—a sense of purpose.

"Chloe mentioned you were making ale. That requires some chemistry, does it not?" She had some knowledge of the process but didn't comprehend the specifics.

"I suppose so." He slid her a glance. "But I consider it more of an art."

Addy spent the next several minutes eking out details of the machinery he used, the part gravity and heat took in the brewing process, and how his ale would contain less alcohol than porters and other ales.

"But I'm boring you." She'd barely noticed that they'd left the park behind until, having arrived at an intersection, he gripped her elbow to keep her from wandering in front of a passing carriage.

"Not at all. I'm more likely to pester you with questions. Who knows when some detail or another might come in handy? Priscilla, Lady Hardwood that is, told me once that I reminded her of a collector. But rather than collecting antiquities, or art, I collected information."

"Likely a good deal more useful."

Addy grimaced. "If not as valuable."

"Now you've got me curious," he said. "Share some tidbit of your collection with me."

It was something she often did with her students, and these tidbits were often met with groans. So to have an avid listener for once, Addy dug into the recesses of her mind for one of her favorites.

"History or science?" she asked.

History.

"Very well. Did you realize that three U.S. presidents died on July 4th, the day of America's birth? There would have been a fourth if James Madison had not declined an offer from his physician to keep him alive until then."

"Jefferson and Adams were two of them," the viscount guessed.

"James Monroe was the third. Madison died on June 28th. His doctor offered to give him stimulants that would keep him alive for six more days, but Madison turned him down."

She laughed. "So, not very useful, really."

"What else do you have?" He sauntered beside her, almost appearing carefree.

Addy scraped her teeth over her bottom lip. "Who was the youngest king ever to rule over England?"

"That's an easy one. Henry the Sixth."

"But do you know how young he was at the time of his accension?" She leaned around so she could see his expression.

"He was an infant," Bloodstone met her stare.

"He was eight months and twenty-six days." And then Addy abandoned her silly facts. "Why have you decided on a lower alcohol content for your ale?"

His eyes lit up. "Because a conscious person can drink more than an unconscious one."

Before they'd made it to the end of the park, they were sharing a lively conversation about the merits of the recent beer act that had been passed by parliament. He'd face more competition because of it, she pointed out. He argued back that it was precisely why he'd spent so much time perfecting his recipes.

He did not gloss over her opinion, however, and answered her questions with the perfect amount of detail.

And it struck Addy that for the first time since arriving in London, she was having an intelligent conversation with a gentleman.

And not just any gentleman.

The most handsome gentleman in all of England.

Lord Bloodstone.

DAMIEN'S DUTY

*D*amien held the door wide for Miss Royal to enter his favorite bakery, Jack's Bread and Biscuits.

He expected the scent of freshly baked bread. He did not expect the surge of heat he felt when Miss Royal brushed by him.

There was something heady about a lady who hid her curves but not her intelligence. No wonder so many of his acquaintances had been felled by these schoolteachers. Damien chuckled to himself, dismissing the notion that he'd be unable to resist such a trap.

If his brewery failed to turn profits enough to keep his estate in the black, Damien would marry one of the ton's favorite debutantes—one with a hefty dowry, of course.

Keeping the estate intact was his primary duty in life. It wasn't as though he had a choice.

Miss Royal, of course, could not be more different than the proper ladies of the ton. The marriageable women in his circle kept their opinions to themselves, giggled softly rather than laugh out loud, and wore heady floral perfumes while this particular schoolteacher's scent wafted sweet and fresh, infused with vanilla and a hint of something he couldn't quite identify—not cinnamon—not ginger.

And if he'd been walking beside a more genteel lady, he'd have had to shorten his strides, whereas Miss Royal, despite her petite frame, had walked with purpose. She had not agreed with everything he said, nor had she tittered at all his jokes. She took deliberate steps, all the while discussing topics other than fashion and the weather.

She was, in fact, a breath of fresh air.

Not that it made any difference to him.

Damien maneuvered them through the orderly half-filled seating area, around tables and chairs until they reached the long glassed-in shelf featuring the day's offerings.

One end held varying types of loaves of bread, but further down, the shelves featured pastries, biscuits, and at the very end, truffles and chocolate conserve.

Miss Royal had released his arm and crossed both of hers in front of herself. She did not step forward, but there was no mistaking her wistful expression.

"Which is your favorite?" Damien urged.

"Anything chocolate, really." Her eyes drifted toward the truffles. "They're awfully dear, aren't they?"

"My treat."

Chocolate. The scent of hers that eluded him was chocolate. He couldn't help but grin at the realization.

Rather than take the time to focus on the scripted cards identifying the choices, he ordered a variety for both along with a pot of tea.

"You mustn't." But her protest was only a mild one, and two minutes later, the two of them were seated at one of the tables adjacent to the windows. From there, they had a perfect view of the park.

Seeing the unmistakable satisfaction she took in each bite, Damien enjoyed watching her more than the pastries themselves.

"This is delicious." She caught him staring and curled her shoulders inward. When it came to academic subjects, she spoke freely, but when she became conscious of herself as a woman, she seemed to intentionally shrink into herself.

Who was her father? The question niggled at the back of his mind. Royal... Surely if her father was of any sort of prominence, he'd have heard of the man.

"Your aunt is a member of the ton. Did she sponsor your come out?" It was possible. But she'd have had to be dowered.

"She did." Miss Royal winced. "I made my come out in the spring of 1824." But she did not elaborate. Obviously, it had not been successful or he wouldn't be sitting with her now.

The bells on the door to the shop jingled, heralding more patrons, and before Damien could ask how she came to be teaching, Miss Royal's eyes flew wide and then she ducked her face into her hands.

"Is that you, Addy? By God, it is you." A male voice carried through the soft murmur of the shop.

Addy? Damien turned to take in the new arrival.

His shoulders were padded and the buttons of his jacket strained to contain his middle. Even though the man's hair was thin and receding, he appeared to be a few years younger than Damien.

The birdlike lady accompanying him wore bright yellow from head to toe and recognized Miss Royal as well. "This is indeed a... surprise. I thought you had taken a teaching position at one of those all-girls schools up north."

Miss Royal dropped her hands into her lap with a forced smile.

"Hello, Miss Kemp, Mr. Banks."

"Oh, but it's Mrs. Banks now. Mr. Banks and I married a few weeks after your... after you cut your season short."

"Felicitations." Miss Royal spoke through stiff lips and turned to Damien. "Forgive me, my lord. Are you acquainted with Mr. and Mrs. Marcus Banks?"

"I've not had the pleasure." Damien rose, curious despite himself.

Looking as though she wished she could disappear into her seat, Miss Royal nonetheless made the proper introductions.

"And how do you know our Addy, my lord?" Mrs. Banks asked.

The lack of respect in their address irritated Damien. "*Miss Royal* is a dear friend of mine."

Banks' mouth twitched as his stare slid back to Miss Royal. "How is your father these days? Still making trouble and insulting his betters?"

A flush crept into Miss Royal's cheeks. "My father is doing well, thank you for asking."

"Our tea grows cold." Damien would discourage drawing out this unpleasant visit.

He would not say it had been a pleasure.

"Say hello to your aunt for me." It was the woman who filled in the awkward silence.

"Of course." Miss Royal seemed to be holding her breath

and only released it after her old acquaintances had excused themselves.

The silence that followed their departure hung thick with unanswered questions.

But before Damien could begin to ask any of them, the small woman in front of him pinched the bridge of her nose. "I thought the ton fled London in the summertime."

"They do." Damien raised his brows. "Ninety-nine percent of them do, anyhow."

"Of all the people I could meet up with... I suppose I'm lucky that way." She popped one of the truffles into her mouth and he noticed her hands were shaking.

"Do you like the cherry ones?" Although mildly curious, Damien would not expect her to discuss what about those two had upset her.

Aside from the obvious, that was.

She required a few seconds to shift topics, but he knew he'd done the right thing when she grinned.

"It's my favorite."

Damien's breath caught to be on the receiving end of her smile. He'd have to feed her more sweets in the future.

On one hand this woman seemed incredibly complicated, and the next, she was a transparent innocent.

"Which kind do you prefer?" she asked.

Rather than answer, Damien reached across the small table to snatch the salted nut truffle. "I hope you didn't want that one."

And there was that smile again

"Two can play at that game." Her eyes sparkled as she mischievously plucked up his cherry-covered truffle, and then popped it into her mouth.

And watching her savor the decadent treat, Damien

could not help but wonder if her lips would taste like cherries now.

Perhaps he ought to rethink his favorite after all.

As soon as the thought jumped into his head, he caught himself. Brushed his hands off and forced his gaze away from her mouth.

"Shall we, then?" he assisted her to her feet and offered his arm. "What did you say your father's name was? Perhaps I can be of some help." The sooner they could leave London and get her back to Miss Primm's, the better it would be for all of them.

"I didn't, did I? But for the record, he is Mr. Charles Royal."

There was something familiar there—it made the back of his neck itch.

Perhaps she came from money after all.

But if she did, why teach?

They made the walk back to Lady Rosewood's townhouse in a comfortable silence but once they arrived, it turned awkward.

"My thanks, again, my lord, for the truffles," she practically stuttered.

"Think nothing of it."

Bending over her hand, he bid her farewell, promising to see what he could do about locating her father.

He didn't expect the tug of disappointment when he turned to make his way home. So much about this woman was unexpected.

The two of them shared more than one mutual acquaintance, therefore, once he deposited her back at the school, they'd meet again.

So he would enjoy her company.

But he'd best exercise more caution.

He was not like his friends, though. He would not fall for the wrong woman. His legacy, he vowed, would always come before his feelings.

THE ANNOUNCEMENT

*A*ddy stepped into the townhouse more than a little disturbed by the afternoon's events.

"I trust you had a pleasant outing?" Mr. Hill, Victoria's butler, asked while assisting with her bonnet and gloves.

"I did." She thanked him despite a heavy feeling in her chest. Her meeting with her aunt had not gone as badly as it could have—and she'd enjoyed most of her time with the viscount.

But she had not been prepared to run into Marcus and Mildred. She'd not foreseen having to face her past.

"Shall I have tea sent up?" Mr. Hill suggested.

"Oh, no," Addy rarely passed on an opportunity to eat, and yet... She shook her head. "No thank you." Even now, the truffles she'd consumed weighed heavy in her belly.

Lord Bloodstone's ability to set a lady at ease had all but swept her off her feet. She would be a fool, however, to imagine she might have charmed him as well. He'd asked questions, and genuinely listened to her answers, but he'd also shared his plans for the brewery while they'd been walking.

And he'd casually mentioned that if it didn't turn out to be as profitable as he hoped, he'd have to seek funds from other avenues. And as a titled Englishman, he no doubt had been speaking of marriage. It was the primary avenue Englishmen took to line their pockets, after all.

Just as long as the bride was in possession of a suitable dowry.

Addy climbed the stairs with leaden feet to the chamber that had been allotted for her. The entire townhouse was lovely, really, despite having fallen into disrepair after Victoria's aunt passed away.

The former owner, much like her own aunt, had lived a somewhat solitary life.

Could Addy do that?

If her father granted her access to what had once been her dowry, would he consider allotting funds for an independent living?

But as she changed out of her gown in the quiet empty room, a hollow feeling opened in her chest. She didn't want to live alone. She didn't want to begin again.

The entire prospect sounded more lonely than it did exciting.

The other teachers at Miss Primm's, along with her students, were more like family to her than any blood-relations ever had been.

What would her life have been like if her mother had lived? Would Addy still fight this shroud of loneliness?

Refusing to wallow in her chamber, however lovely it might be, Addy donned a more comfortable gown and made her way downstairs to the library. Victoria had boasted that it was the first room she'd renovated after inheriting the townhouse from her aunt, and she'd not only spent money on the furnishing, but on restoring some of the content and updating it with new.

Addy stepped inside with a sense of reverence. Noting that the wood gleamed, she inhaled the scent that she'd never quite figured out how to describe.

Not chocolate, or vanilla or coffee—but... age. Older books smelled different than new ones.

She inhaled the musty smell, holding it in her lungs, and then released it back into the quiet room.

Like a giant tree that had fallen in the woods, the bound paper was already decomposing. How could it not, affected by air and moisture and... humans?

She trailed her fingertips along the shelf as she examined a few titles. Currently caught up in Holden Hampden's latest work of fiction, all she required was a quiet place to sit.

But just as she settled into one of the plush armchairs, she spotted a copy of the London Gazette sitting on a round mahogany table beside her. Not ready to lose herself in reading quite yet, she plucked up the newspaper and unfolded its neatly ironed pages.

Primm had a subscription mailed to her regularly, but Addy hadn't taken much time to peruse it in the past. Today, however, she was practically on holiday.

She glanced over an article proposing reform, news of this autumn's coronation, and a few pages in, a column of social announcements.

The Marquess of Dillingham had died in a carriage accident, and... a secret wedding had taken place in London.

Addy paused, her brow furrowed.

Had some reporter gotten wind of Chloe and Captain Edgeworth's hasty marriage?

Two names popped out at her, and they were not Edgeworth's and Chloe's.

"The Viscount Bloodstone and Miss Adelaide Royal..."

She had to read the announcement at least five times before she could convince herself that she was not imagining it.

The Gazette, for reasons beyond her comprehension, had incorrectly reported the participants of the secret wedding.

They wrote that one of England's most sought-after bachelors, the Viscount Bloodstone, had been snatched up.

By none other than the Mad American's daughter: Miss Adelaide Elizabeth Royal.

HIS LORDSHIP, *Damien Reddington of Reddington Park, was seen leaving the church with none other than the only daughter of Mr. Charles Royal, known as the Mad American. Miss Adelaide Royal left society a few weeks into her season following her failed engagement to Mr. Marcus Banks of Mayfair. Mr. Banks, it is said, made a hasty escape when the Mad American cancelled his daughter's dowry only days before the wedding.*

Following a dispute with the Duke of Pinkerton, the Mad American vowed never to pay a single pound to any of England's nobility, cancelling out his daughter's dowry, and effectively ending the chit's marriage contract.

Is it possible the Mad American has recanted his penny-pinching vow? Why else would the esteemed Viscount Bloodstone shackle himself to a virtual nobody?

. . .

INACCURACIES ASIDE, the reporter had unfairly exposed Addy's scandal all over again.

She had no idea how long she sat staring at the paper. Addy was stunned into numbness initially, but as the reality of it eventually sank in, questions began ricocheting around in her brain.

How was this possible?

Why would the reporter write such nonsense?

And most importantly, what could they do to make it go away?

BAD NEWS

*D*amien squinted down at what he'd just written but then lost his focus when a knock sounded.

"Pardon, my lord," his butler, Mr. Smith, peered into the study. "A young woman is here to see you."

Damien glanced toward the window where darkness had fallen nearly an hour before. There was only one young woman who knew he was in Mayfair right now.

"Miss Royal," Mr. Smith supplied before Damien could ask.

Perhaps her father had made his appearance already—allotted her the money she requested—and she wished to leave Mayfair first thing in the morning.

But why not just send Damien a missive? Her showing up on his doorstep, alone, at such a late hour, was the height of impropriety.

And dangerous—to not only her reputation but also his bachelorhood.

Damien shoved the papers away for now. He couldn't

send her away, not after having claimed responsibility for her.

So he simply waited, and when she entered his study, the hair on the back of his neck pricked up.

She'd changed into a different gown than the one she had been wearing this morning. It was lighter, the pale mint not as somber as the muslin she'd worn to visit her aunt.

But the springy pastel was the only thing calming about her. Her cheeks were flushed a deep scarlet, her green eyes flashed, and half her hair had escaped from what had once been a formally neat chignon.

The first thought Damien had was that she brought some life to this house. The second was that for her to appear, looking like this, she must be in some sort of trouble.

He rose, his thoughts shooting to a myriad of possibilities as to what could have brought her here. "Miss Royal."

More than a glimmer of panic sparked in her eyes.

She held up a paper: The London Gazette. "I don't know how it happened. Have you seen it? It wasn't us. It was Chloe and Captain Edgeworth. They can fix this, can't they?"

"What is it?" What the devil was she going on about?

Before he could step around to get a closer look, Miss Royal had opened the paper and was smoothing it open on the surface of his desk.

"Look here," she pointed and then took a self-conscious step backward. In the dancing candlelight, the columns of small, printed letters appeared more scrambled than usual.

He'd had a long day, filled with note-taking and paper-work and business correspondence. By now it was a struggle to maintain his focus.

He squeezed the bridge of his nose and sighed. "Why don't you just tell me."

She stared at him with narrowed eyes, but then stepped back up to the paper.

"This says that it was you and I who were married." She leaned forward, dragging her fingertip along a line that did, in fact, jump out to Damien, and proceeded to read aloud. *"Dear reader, this reporter has learned that Damien Reddington, Viscount Bloodstone, secretly wed himself to the daughter of the Mad American, Miss Adelaide Elizabeth Royal, early Friday morning of this week at St. Michael's chapel on Shaftesbury Avenue.*

"His lordship, Damien Reddington of Reddington Park was seen leaving the church..." She paused and rubbed her hand down her face. "Why would they do this?"

She'd worked herself into quite a state.

Forcing his stare back to the paper, Damien managed to focus enough to read through the remainder of the article.

And conceded that she was upset with good reason.

Not only had the reporter totally misreported the facts, but he'd also managed to drag up her past engagement as well.

No wonder she'd been so distraught at the bakery today, she'd come face to face with the blighter who'd jilted her.

And her father, by God, was the Mad American. Of course, he'd heard of the man. He simply had not made the connection.

But that was the least of their concerns.

He frowned at the article.

Of all the scandals he'd ever imagined himself in, this was one he'd never considered.

But... Surely, it wasn't something that could not be

undone. It wasn't as though he and Miss Royal had done anything wrong.

"Why would they do this?" Her voice trembled as she pondered the question again. She'd sidled up beside him and he got a whiff of her intriguing perfume—sweet and clean—not unlike the wearer.

But he was shaking his head. "It's a mistake. They will print a retraction." Surely that would resolve the matter?

"But what if people read the announcement and miss the retraction? What about my students' parents? What about Miss Primm's? Does this mean I'm ruined?"

Her questions unfurled an unsettling sensation in his chest.

"Definitely not. You've done nothing wrong. We've done nothing wrong. It's simply a misunderstanding." A *very public* misunderstanding.

"Isn't that how half the ton gets ruined? By being caught in some sort of misunderstanding?"

"It's not as though we ran off to Gretna Green. And no one has caught us alone together." Damien glanced toward the door and then back to her. Their eyes locked knowingly. "Yet."

Because her simply being in his study, late at night like this, was compromising in itself.

"The key to keeping out of trouble is not getting caught," he added.

She was the one nodding now, albeit, with a wince. "Right. Right. I know I shouldn't have come, but I couldn't sit around and do nothing. We need a plan. What do we do now? We need to do something!"

Tension vibrated off her. Tiny lines formed on her forehead and her hands were shaking.

If he were at home, he'd go to his mother or Hardwood's mother for advice. Either would know the best way to remedy this situation. Trouble was, in regard to maneuvering through the web of society's strict but sometimes nonsensical rules, all he'd ever paid heed to was how to hide indiscretions. He'd never considered that he might have to defend...

He flicked his stare back to the paper.

This.

Resisting the urge to bury his head in his hands, the ramifications of their circumstances grew heavier as reality set in.

As a bachelor, he'd done his damnedest to prevent his name being linked with any one particular debutante—because that was how trouble began.

A public wedding announcement did just that; it linked his name with Miss Royal's—a woman whose father had vowed he'd never pay one farthing out for her dowry—especially not to an English Lord.

And marrying well was his backup plan. Not having that option would mean he had no choice but to make a success of the brewery.

But he was getting the cart before the horses.

Another wince.

"She could, but it's in her interest to have a niece connected to a viscount. I'm not at all certain she'll feel compelled to, er, disconnect me."

Damien watched Miss Royal's expression carefully and a suspicious thought began to take root. Was it possible that she was the person who'd sent word to the Gazette?

Had she tired of having to teach for a living? At some point, she might very well have realized that being "compromised" by him might be a once-in-a-lifetime opportunity. Without a dowry, she had little to no options otherwise.

"Did you know about this?" he asked.

Her eyes flew open wide. "Surely, you're not implying that I—? I would never!" Her hands were shaking even more now. "How could you even think such a thing?"

"I don't know *what* to think."

He strode across the room and stared into the fireless hearth. She'd tried shedding his protection ever since Edgeworth and Miss Fortune's ceremony. To think she'd perpetrate such a scheme was reaching, at best.

He dismissed the suspicion as easily as he'd grasped hold of it.

"My apologies, Miss Royal." Of course she hadn't been the person to contact the Gazette.

She had thrown the flowers. And then he'd tossed some coin. The gestures had seemed harmless at the time— amusing even.

But they must be the events that had inspired the announcement.

"The flowers!" She must have been reading his mind.

"And the coins," he added.

Still, any reporter worth his salt ought to have checked the church registry before writing up a damned announcement. The paper ought to require proof before running such an unlikely story.

"I'm going to the Gazette's offices first thing in the morning."

He glanced back to where she was standing—leaning against the desk almost as though her legs couldn't hold her up. Guilt pricked at him.

Voicing those suspicions had tipped her onto the verge of tears.

Which, he conceded, were quite unexceptional under such circumstances.

Damien glanced around the room.

He was going to have to take quick action to keep her from falling apart.

"I don't blame you," he stepped toward her. "You cannot have known a reporter was looking on."

"But I threw the flowers." She swiped a hand over her eyes. "Only brides throw flowers. It was a stupid, stupid thing to do! I should have known better."

"I threw the coins. This is as much my fault as yours."

She was shaking. Her hands had trembled earlier today at the pastry shop—when that Banks fellow had appeared.

"But what do we do now?" She looked to him for an answer.

Not having one, Damien eased her into his arms. It was something he'd do for his sister—or for his mother.

"Everything will work out," he assured her, taking care to keep his voice level.

He ought not to have found her scent tantalizing.

He ought not to appreciate how perfectly she fit against him—soft to hard, yin to yang.

Damien rubbed his hands down her back. His thoughts, especially at a time such as this, ought to be brotherly. *He'd promised to protect her.*

"On the off chance that your aunt is sympathetic, I think you ought to consult with her first thing in the morning."

She nodded her head beneath his chin. "I'm s-s-sorry. Of course."

"It's only a little article. And with half of London's residents in the country, it's unlikely anyone's even seen it."

One could always hope.

One could always dream.

Another nod, and a forced smile.

"Aunt Georgia is wise to the ways of the ton." Miss Royal drew back, blinking and looking confused all over again as she wiggled free.

"But the rest of the article—the old scandal involving my father... What can I do about that?"

"SHE'LL NEVER MARRY"

*A*ddy felt sick inside. It wasn't fair that this be raked up again.

Lord Bloodstone's jaw pulsed. "Your father is rather notorious. If I'd realized…" He shook his head. "No wonder Banks upset you…"

"Yes, well…" Addy exhaled. "I never should have returned to Mayfair."

"It was Banks who jilted you? Because of your father?" The viscount had to have heard of the Mad American Royal —of course he had.

But it had been a long time ago.

And their last name, Royal, had dropped off the nickname in no time at all.

"My father is a gambling man. Second to making money, I'm convinced it's his favorite pursuit. And when he wins, he expects his opponents to pay up." Addy took a deep breath, gathering herself. It was in the past, but still not something she preferred to discuss.

Unable to hold his gaze, she raised her eyes to the ceiling, blinking back further tears as she continued, "When the Duke of Pinkerton attempted to pawn off a vowel instead of the money he owed, my father was livid. Society backed the duke, of course, and my father declared that no aristocrat would ever see a farthing of his fortune—and that included my dowry."

Addy exhaled a loud sigh. The implications of her father's vendetta had lit a fire under all of society—metaphorically speaking. But amidst all the drama, it wasn't her father who suffered the repercussions, and it certainly hadn't been the duke.

No, her father's declaration had affected Addy more than anyone else.

It had meant the end of her betrothal and subsequently, all but gotten her shunned by her aunt.

Thank heavens for Primm.

Lord Bloodstone stood with folded arms and simply studied her. "I'd say you made a lucky escape."

Addy shot a quick glance at the open newspaper. "It didn't feel like it at the time."

Especially because she'd been one of the last to know.

A lucky escape... Damien's words summoned a vivid memory of that fateful last night.

Addy had liked her fiancé very much. She'd hoped she would someday love him.

Even her aunt had been happy, declaring the engagement a triumph. Marcus was a respected and handsome gentleman, but he was also the son of a baron.

And strolling amongst the guests at the Harborton's Ball, Addy had felt relatively confident. She and Marcus had been engaged for two weeks. She'd succeeded in landing a husband where more-refined debutantes had not.

The night had been a warm one, although not as uncomfortable as tonight. Left to her own devices, Addy had procured a glass of lemonade for herself and then lingered behind some potted plants as she watched for her fiancé's arrival.

"Miss Royal cannot be surprised to lose him—not after her father's actions. She is a nobody." A voice had sounded from the opposite side of the ornamental tree. *"No one will blame Mr. Banks—not without a dowry in play. He's made a lucky escape in my opinion."*

And then a second voice had added salt to the wound.

"Mr. Banks would be an excellent match for my niece. Her dowry's not as hefty as some but it ought to be enough to bring his estate back into the black. He's dancing with her now, you know."

Addy had gone numb as she listened. She'd not been able to locate Marcus yet. Had he been avoiding her? The gossip couldn't be true and yet...

She had known her father was acting improperly—that he'd created something of a scandal. How could she not? But Marcus had told her he loved her.

He'd told her she was the woman of his dreams.

"Miss Royal is ruined, of course. She'll never marry."

The glass of lemonade had slipped from Addy's lifeless fingers onto the marble floor. The shattering crash had exposed her.

She'd recognized the women who turned around immediately. Mrs. Kemp, Mrs. Possum and Lady Shilling. They had shown zero humility or regret at having discussed her with such a lack of discretion.

"Where did you hear that?" Addy asked. *"You're joking, aren't you?"* Only, deep down in her heart, she'd known the truth.

Her father had made himself into a pariah. And in doing that, he'd made her into one as well.

"Miss Royal?" Lord Bloodstone had reached out and was squeezing her hand. "Why didn't your father simply return to America? If he had such animosity for English ways."

Why didn't he...? She blinked, forcing herself to return to the present.

She shook her head. "He'd already moved his business to Europe. He'd sold his mines in the Carolinas and invested in his shipping company."

Addy had not allowed herself to dwell on that night for a very long time. Sometimes if she couldn't sleep, or if she was feeling low, the memory crept into her thoughts to haunt her.

But seeing Marcus—seeing him with Mildred Kemp—brought everything back.

And now, to have it shared again so publicly...

"I'm sorry you had to go through that."

A more sophisticated lady would wave a hand through the air, dismissing her feelings. She would laugh about it, agreeing that she'd made a lucky escape. But Addy, well...

She craved a cherry-covered truffle.

She swallowed and then met the viscount's beautiful blue eyes. "He didn't even have the courage to tell me himself."

"You were ruined," he stated.

"I was lucky Miss Primm took me on." Addy pulled her hand out of his. "But enough about my sad past. We have more pressing issues to address."

"Indeed." His jaw pulsed again and the sound of the clock ticking on the mantle became noticeable.

Lord Bloodstone stepped back, putting an appropriate distance between them.

Suddenly gone was the sympathetic gentleman from a few moments ago, in his place an aloof stranger. "We'll squash any rumors as quickly as possible." He cleared his throat. "I can't marry without a dowry. We need to be more careful in the future." His voice sounded grim but determined.

Addy wouldn't reveal that she'd never marry without a dowry. She'd not do that to any gentleman.

And not out of any sense of honor, but because she would never make herself into such a burden. She'd been a liability to her father for most of her life, and then to her aunt.

She refused to add to the burden of some titled Englishman.

And she was not without skills. She was not without means.

She was not without a level of pride.

"I'll leave." She moved toward the door.

"How did you get here?"

"Coachman John," she answered. "He's waiting for me outside."

His unease was almost palpable. "You shouldn't come here alone."

Her first instinct was to bristle indignantly, but he had good reason to be concerned.

The very identifiable coach, visible for all the world to see outside his townhouse, would only provide more fodder for any gossips who might have remained in town.

He was right, of course he was right. The two of them needed to step carefully from here on out. The announcement hadn't really been their fault, but that didn't mean they wouldn't misstep in the future.

Best to exercise better judgment from here on.

Then again, the best judgment in the world couldn't trump bad luck.

SOME INCLEMENT WEATHER

After experiencing a mostly sleepless night, Addy rose at dawn the next morning and waited impatiently for a reasonable hour when she could make a second visit to her aunt.

And although she tried reading, her thoughts persistently returned to the evening before.

Lord Bloodstone had taken her into his arms.

After accusing her of trying to trap him!

But it had almost been worth it.

She couldn't remember the last time she'd felt protected, comfortable, safe. With a father who thrived on risk, the notion of wellbeing, of belonging, wasn't a familiar one.

For that short time when he'd tucked her head beneath his chin, Lord Bloodstone had almost made her feel as though she mattered.

Sitting in Victoria's library, sipping tea and watching the sun rise, she replayed the sensation of his arms pulling her into his chest. His scent ought to have been exotic and strange, but it had felt... familiar. Cedar and spice had made up a warm fragrance she'd wanted to imprint on her memory forever.

Foolishness.

He'd thought she was going to cry. She'd seen his wince before he'd done whatever was necessary to prevent a bout of tears.

When the clock finally struck ten, deciding she'd waited long enough, Addy tied on her bonnet and, dodging Coachman John this time, walked the short distance to her aunt's.

But her bad luck hadn't run out yet.

Her aunt had departed for Bath very early that morning.

Had she even bothered trying to contact Addy's father for her? Unsuccessful at wringing any additional information from her aunt's loyal butler, Addy returned to Victoria's townhouse to regroup.

She'd had no choice but to seek out Lord Bloodstone the night before, but she would refrain from doing so again.

Leaving her with no choice but to wait to hear from him.

He'd said he'd find a way to resolve this. He'd demand the retraction and any potential scandal would resolve itself.

Meanwhile, all she had to do was sit here.

And wait.

She didn't have to wait long.

***

"What do you mean, they want proof? How does one go about proving that they are *not* married? Is there some sort of certificate one can obtain stating just that?" Addy asked.

She'd known he brought bad news when she got her first

look at him as he was escorted into the library. He'd looked immaculate, of course, in his buff breeches, starched shirt, pristine cravat and black coat. His lavender waistcoat appeared to have been selected for how well it matched his eyes.

But aside from all that, his hair stood out at a few odd angles as though he'd been running his fingers through it, and a scowl marred his beautiful mouth.

Addy could almost imagine him growling as he stalked around Victoria's withdrawing room.

Like a lion.

The man did not stand still in the face of a challenge.

"The editor is an imbecile. The facts, he said, came from one of their most trusted sources. I asked him why on earth I would need to hide such information if it was in fact, true, and all he could respond with was that he never understood why nobs did most of the things they did."

Lord Bloodstone marched back across the room and halted at her side. "So, having no luck there, I naturally returned to the church to see about a statement from the priest." He threw his hands in the air. "Closed. But of course. Apparently, priests take holidays along with the rest of us."

"It was locked?"

"Tighter than Newgate."

"But...that's ridiculous!" Addy paced across the room this time. "If I were the editor of a major newspaper, I would happily correct any mistakes made by my reporters."

"You and me both, Miss Royal." But then he turned. "Did you have any luck with your aunt?"

"She left town early this morning." It was possible her aunt had left without even reading the article. Had she even intended to send word to her father? Addy and her father represented scandal.

Aunt Georgia hated scandal more than anything.

"There's only one thing left for us to do." Addy folded her arms with a frown.

"I... I've already told you... I can't—" He looked as though he might lose the contents of his stomach.

And yet he still managed to look incredibly handsome. It really wasn't fair.

"Not that." She scoffed. Good lord, he'd thought she was going to demand he make her an offer. "We need to go to Miss Primm," she said, sending his brows into his hairline. Addy would have laughed at his expression if their circumstances weren't quickly becoming dire. "For as long as I've known her, she's had the answer to everything."

Not only had Primm saved Addy from having to take work in a less than optimal circumstance, and nearly every other teacher she employed, but she'd managed to keep the school afloat despite a deluge of scandals.

If anyone would know what to do in these circumstances, it was Miss Primm.

"What about your father?" he turned his head to stare out the window. It was almost as though mentioning her father had summoned the threatening clouds outside. The day promised to be dark, rainy, and depressing.

"I'll ask him about the other issue later." It was possible he was on a ship somewhere in the middle of the Indian Ocean. Of course, he could also just as easily be transacting business down on the dock. Either way, getting money for Miss Primm's was going to have to wait.

And she and Lord Bloodstone were going to have to make haste.

She glanced around the room and shivered. Victoria's townhouse had felt a little lonely since Chloe moved out, but it had been comfortable. And it had felt safe. No one had questioned her right to be there.

"So you want to go back to the school now?" he asked.

"I don't think we have a choice."

"I'll tell your coachman," he said. He must be anxious indeed to shed himself of the fictional wife the Gazette had written for him.

But he was right. There was no reason for them to remain in Mayfair. In fact, the sooner they were away from curious eyes, the better.

**

Addy stared out the window, looking down where rain pelted the road. Unfortunately, neither of them had accounted for England's volatile weather.

They'd passed the gates to the city less than an hour before, and she wondered if perhaps they shouldn't have waited after all. Lightning flashed and thunder followed almost instantly and from where she sat she could make out tiny rivers carving edges into the road.

Poor Coachman John would be drenched already, as would Lord Bloodstone, who had chosen to ride outside.

For days on end, now, they had all suffered the smothering and oppressive heat in town. Less than half a day's drive out, and already the rain had lowered the temperature considerably.

Watching his progress through the window, Addy's breath caught when thunder cracked again, causing Lord Bloodstone's horse to rear back. If it hadn't been so terrifying, the sight of the viscount managing the black beast would have been magnificent. As it was, she didn't breathe normally again until she saw that he'd brought the horse back under control.

But not a minute later, the carriage jerked and turned, sending Addy flying across the bench against the opposite wall before Coachman John righted them.

The careening sensation reminded her of the crossing from America—one particular storm had roared on for nearly two days.

On a ship, there was no stopping. No disembarking.

Trusting that her coachman would keep them safe, and that Lord Bloodstone was watching over them as well, Addy tightened her shawl around her shoulders with one hand and braced herself for another slide with the other. They skidded again but now she was prepared for it.

Moments later, however, the coach slowed to a halt and men's voices rose above the sounds of the storm, likely discussing their options.

Any minute, she expected the small sliding door to the driver's box to open and for Coachman John to inform her they would be turning around.

Instead, the door to the carriage itself flew open. Along with a very wet gust of wind, Lord Bloodstone's grim face filled the opening.

"Mind if I join you?"

He clutched his top hat in front of him, and his blond hair looked darker, slicked back on his head like a seal. He might just as well have emerged from a swimming pond or bath, with water on his lashes and clinging to his upper lip.

"Not at all." While he maneuvered himself inside, Addy moved from the front-facing bench to the back facing one.

Her breaths became shorter and her heart raced as his presence filled the small interior. No matter how many times she tried to ignore his effect on her, she had yet to gain control of it.

It was silly, really. The stuff of naïve schoolgirls. Regardless, there were more significant matters to be dealt with.

Even if anyone had actually read the announcement in the paper, those with half a brain would know it couldn't be true. Men like Lord Bloodstone simply didn't marry ladies such as herself.

Not deliberately, anyhow.

"My apologies," he settled, and then, upon realizing that she'd given up her spot, said, "you needn't sit backwards."

Addy was shaking her head. "It doesn't bother me."

Best to keep her distance.

With his broad shoulders and impressive height, he was imposing enough while walking beside her in the park, or standing at the hearth in her drawing room. In the confines of the carriage, however, his being there sucked the air out of the vehicle.

"There's a small village about an hour up ahead. If this doesn't let up by then, we'll stop there."

"What about your horse?"

"Chaos?" He shook his head. "I dismounted to check her leg and she took off without me."

Addy blinked, surprised. "You've lost her?"

But he didn't seem overly concerned.

"She'll come back. She's done this before."

"I hope so." Addy bit into her bottom lip. "She's a beautiful mount."

"She is," he agreed. And then, "And she will." He ran a

hand down his face, drawing her attention back to his bedraggled condition.

His greatcoat was sopping wet. For an instant, the sight took her back to a long-ago afternoon when she'd travelled from Raleigh to Philadelphia with her father. Her father's meetings had been cancelled and the bumps in the road had made it impossible for him to read his contracts.

It had been one of the rare occasions when she'd had her father's undivided attention.

Blinking away the unexpected memory, she reached forward. "You should get out of this before you catch your death," she said. He hesitated just a moment before turning and allowing her to assist him out of the bulky garment and drape it on the seat beside her.

His wool jacket beneath the coat was damp, but less so.

That day in the rain, her father had stripped down to his shirt and waistcoat. He'd never been the sort of person to care for propriety or rules.

Another shock of lightning flashed in the windows.

"My father isn't mad." The words spilled out of her mouth without her having planned them. It must have been the combination of having come to London, of having talked with her aunt, and now this particular memory.

But she wanted Lord Bloodstone to know.

The viscount simply stared across the carriage at her. "Of course he isn't."

Was he only agreeing with her to avoid upsetting her again? She'd gone nine years without hearing from her father. Why, then, did she feel the need to defend him?

Simple.

He was her father.

"He is a hard worker—he's always worked harder than

anyone I know. He's smart and driven, and very, *very* much American. But he isn't mad."

To imply that he was mad suggested something was wrong with his brain. He might perhaps chase after industry and capital more than was strictly necessary, and he never failed to hold his tongue, but that didn't make him a bad person.

And it certainly didn't mean he was fit for Bedlam.

In for a penny, in for a pound. "He never knew who his father was," she said. "And his mother died when he was just a boy. But he didn't settle. He fought his way out of poverty. He defied the odds and has since built his business into a small empire." Her father had made a life for himself, and for her, out of nothing—going so far as to make up his own name.

Royal.

He'd told her once that he'd never known his own father's surname. Given the opportunity to come up with his own, he'd reached for the stars.

And his blood ran in her veins. Adelaide Elizabeth Royal.

If he was mad, then what was she?

Bumping along the now-rutted road, Addy waited for the viscount to contradict her. But no argument came. Instead, he tilted his head patiently, allowing her to speak her piece.

"I just wanted you to know that," she finished.

And then he took the wind out of her sails by answering, "Of course he isn't mad."

"But you'd heard of him? Before I mentioned who my father was," she speculated.

"I had."

"It's just that my father is very literal. He sees the world

73

in terms of blacks or whites—plusses or minuses. And his mind is always working—or it was when I last saw him. He's always looking for a way to capitalize on some need or another. He believes a man's handshake is his promise, and that promises ought to be golden." More lightning flashed, and if anything, the rain fell even harder.

"He is right to expect that," the viscount said. "Trouble is, we are not in America. He chose to come to England; he should have known he'd be expected to abide by English rules. Furthermore, the man he challenged was a duke. You ought to have realized that in London, dukes do no wrong. Your father began a war he could never win."

"Do you think that's right?"

"It doesn't matter what I think. It's the world we live in."

Addy swallowed hard. "I don't like it."

Lord Bloodstone responded to that with a quiet chuckle. "I wouldn't expect you to. You're the person who's carried the burden for it."

What was he saying?

"I'm sorry it landed on you. It's not fair you had to suffer."

Addy held his gaze, heat burning behind her eyes.

She'd known this all along, and yet not one person had ever directly expressed this to her—not her aunt, not her father—not even Miss Primm.

Because when one looked at the facts, for a single turn of cards that transpired between some old duke and Addy's father, Addy had been the one who'd paid the most.

She'd paid with her dignity.

With her pride.

With her future.

Lucky for her, she'd not lost her heart.

"DID I HURT YOU?"

$\mathcal{K}$nowing his mount would find her way back to them, Damien had climbed inside the carriage, not to remove himself from the rain, but to ensure Miss Royal wasn't afraid. More than once, the coach had skidded and then slid side to side.

Damien reclined against the bench. He was more than a little surprised at the turn their conversation had taken.

It intrigued him, though, that she would defend her father so passionately. Mr. Royal couldn't be more different than his own father had been.

The man who'd sired Damien had lived to meet propriety's demands. He'd worn the latest fashions, read the right books, appreciated the popular artists of the day, and said all the right things while in public.

The prior Lord Bloodstone had treated his wife with dignity and raised his children to do the same, and nothing had mattered more than his reputation and standing.

Unfortunately, Damien's father had accomplished all of

this while accruing a mountain of debt, ignoring the disrepair of his estate.

A few more years, and he would have squandered his legacy in its entirety.

Their legacy.

Even so, Damien wouldn't have traded his father for the world.

Miss Royal, who was nodding, seemed to feel the same for the man who'd sired her.

He'd yet to have seen her shed a single tear but Damien sensed a cauldron of emotions inside her. So much so that he could almost imagine steam rolling off her.

"But look at you now," he winked. "Married to a viscount."

She brushed her hair out of her face with a shaking hand. "You know I didn't—"

"I know." Damien clenched his fists.

He'd taken her into his arms once already, the night before when she'd risked coming alone to his townhouse.

And now, she sat less than a foot away from him looking far too vulnerable.

Far too… *kissable,* damnit.

He forced his stare away from her mouth.

The trouble was, he needed to protect his own interests as well. If he stood any chance at remaining unmarried—while maintaining his honor—he needed to act with all due respectability.

"We're lucky this isn't the summer of sixteen," she changed the subject.

"The year without a summer."

"My father didn't mind." She grimaced. "From what I've heard, it wasn't nearly as bad in America as it was in

Europe, so I don't really remember living through it. But I've heard my father talk enough to feel as though I was right there. The industrialist in him realized the ramifications and invested in sources of grain and flour. To this day, he claims he made more in those two years than a decade of mining."

Her shaking subsided as she spoke.

She clutched her arms in front of her, unintentionally drawing his gaze to where she'd pushed her bosom up.

When she shivered, Damien handed over his jacket, which had been mostly kept dry beneath his greatcoat.

"Thank you."

Damien dragged his gaze up to hers. "You don't need to thank me for anything."

"But I—"

Whatever she'd meant to say was cut off when the coach lurched hard, sending her flying off the bench onto the floor, her face slamming into his lap uncomfortably close to sensitive organs.

Damien tightened his arms around her until the ride levelled out, waiting for Coachman John to pull them to a halt for a broken wheel or axel.

"Are you hurt?" With his face dipped down near her ear, her fragrance drew him closer. "Miss Royal?" His voice came out more strained sounding than usual.

"I'm fine." She squirmed until he'd loosened his grip. "Did I hurt you? I'm terribly sorry—"

"No." She had nothing to be sorry for.

The carriage bounced again at the same moment she attempted to lean back onto her knees, and when she fell forward this time, he was prepared to catch her.

No doubt Coachman John was pushing them intentionally, anxious that they arrive in the next village before the roads became impassable.

"Sit here beside me." Damien pulled her onto the seat, not giving her a chance to crawl to the opposite bench. For such a small and rounded woman, she certainly possessed sharp elbows.

"Well," she said, upright again, albeit with the security of his arm around her shoulders. "That was unexpected."

It had been.

Not only the violence of the jostling ride, but his reluctance to remove his arm from around her.

For her safety?

For his?

Or for some other reason?

Under most circumstances, he had no difficulty controlling himself—both his internal reactions and his external response.

And yet, on more than one occasion, this small woman had managed to slip under his skin.

She possessed an intangible combination of independence and vulnerability, naivete and intelligence, and both contradictions ignited his... protective instincts.

"But you mustn't worry about me. I'm not afraid," she said.

"Good." A study in contrasts to be certain—terrified for Miss Primm's School, yet a bastion of strength traveling through this epic summer storm. "We'll be fine, then."

She glanced over, looking more than a little doubtful.

"What?" Damien cocked a brow.

"Do you really believe we can extricate ourselves from this... situation?" She was not talking about the rain. "I find it impossible to comprehend that the Gazette would run something so obviously false."

"Why obviously false?"

"Because," she pulled her shoulders inward as though to make herself smaller. "Because you are you and I am me…"

"But you are an unmarried lady, who is both intelligent and lovely." The compliment seemed to make her uncomfortable. "And I am quite a catch, if I do say so myself."

There was that smile, reluctant, but a smile nonetheless.

"We'll be fine," he answered her other question. "Off the top of my head, I can think of a handful of others who've faced worse scandals than this one and emerged with their reputations intact."

"Such as?"

Easy.

"Hardwood and Miss Fellowes, for starters. Good lord, she impersonated one of her students! And look at Captain Edgeworth and your friend, Miss Fortune!"

"Both of those couples are married now."

True. Damien scratched his chin. Come to think of it, as he contemplated names of gentlemen he'd come of age with, Chaswick, the Ravensdale brothers, even the Duke of Blackheart…

All the bachelors who'd entangled themselves had had to resort to…

Marriage.

Blast.

But it was of no matter. His and Miss Royal's circumstances were of a different nature entirely. "Not to worry, though. You and I have done nothing wrong," he insisted.

And it would remain that way as long as one discounted

the fact that she'd come to his house alone late at night, and that he was currently riding alone with her in this carriage.

But no one need ever learn about either of these indiscretions.

Unfortunately, the unavoidable indiscretions had only just begun...

VISCOUNTS DON'T SLEEP ON FLOORS

"*I*t's your lucky day, Mr. Reddington," the scruffy innkeeper behind the counter announced. "We happen to have two chambers left."

Addy glanced around the rundown-looking tap room while the viscount signed the register.

Lord Bloodstone, who was signing on the allotted lines, had told her he would not use his title. And to keep anyone from asking questions, he'd refer to her as his wife.

Since no one would recognize either of them here, they'd decided together that such a fabrication was the best route to take to avoid unnecessary speculation. When she'd suggested she pretend to be his sister, he'd waved the suggestion away.

Because she was obviously American, and he was obviously… not.

Not as familiar with such matters, she willingly went along with the pretense, watching with casual interest as her fictitious husband very deliberately formed each letter.

While he paid, she diverted her attention to the door

that had blown open, ushering in a burst of rain along with a tired-looking couple with two small children.

The man, whose red hair matched both of the children's, hobbled in to stand behind Addy while the lady shuffled the bedraggled boy and girl over to the hearth. Addy's stomach clenched.

The small girl stood shivering, drenched and with mud coming up to her knees, while the boy lowered himself to his haunches, holding his hands toward the fire.

"You'll have to move along, I'm afraid." The innkeeper informed the new arrivals. "We're all filled up!"

The woman shot her husband an almost terrified glance, raising her hand to her mid-section. Addy's heart squeezed. Because if she was not incorrect, the lady was with child.

"Don't you have anything, sir? We were forced to leave our cart a few miles down the road—sunk three feet into the mud. We've been walking for hours, and I don't think the children or my wife can make it any further. Can we bed down in your stables, sir, just until this storm passes?"

Addy's heart squeezed. This poor family's struggles all but eradicated the dire nature of her and Lord Bloodstone's troubles.

"I suppose." The innkeeper frowned and his stare landed on the boy. "But keep the little ones away from the horses."

Addy imagined the four of them trying to warm up outside in the stables. The mother would not be able to change her children out of their wet clothing. They wouldn't have mattresses to lie down on, or blankets for warmth.

It wouldn't do. She could not allow it. This was, she decided, a life-or-death situation.

"They can have one of our rooms," Addy announced and

then met Lord Bloodstone's gaze. "You don't mind, do you, Mr. Reddington, *dear?*"

He raised one of his brows but didn't contradict her. "Not at all, *darling.*" He handed one of the keys back to the innkeeper. "But leave both rooms on my bill."

His words warmed Addy from the inside.

Lord Bloodstone was a *good* man.

"That's not necessary, sir," the father of the small brood held up a hand. His grimace revealed an internal struggle between his need and his pride.

But the wife did not suffer similarly.

"My humble thanks to you, sir. Your generosity is most appreciated," the woman shot her husband a chastising glance, and a grateful one to Addy. "Thank you," she said.

A few minutes later, with all the rooms and keys sorted out, Lord Bloodstone excused himself to ask around the stables after his mount, while Addy climbed the stairs in search of their room. She immediately noticed thick cobwebs clinging to the corners of the ceiling, and she kept her hands to herself to avoid the grime on the walls.

The interior of their small chamber wasn't much of an improvement.

A musty smell hung in the air, and dirt streaked the pane of the single window where ants crawled along the sill.

But the patchwork quilt on the bed looked thick and inviting, and the mattress appeared to be relatively level.

Having taken stock, she shed her damp coat and struck the flint to the hearth in the corner.

She and Lord Bloodstone were dry, Coachman John was out of the elements, and their carriage was safely tucked away in the mews. And...

The door opened.

And she was going to share a room with a man who was not really her husband.

"Oh, my lord." He had mud halfway up his breeches and was even more soaked than he'd been before.

"Are you 'my lording' me, or the weather?" The viscount cocked a brow with a smirk.

Rain rolled off his hair and hung in drops on the wool of his coat. Addy stepped forward without so much as hesitating.

"Both," she huffed, helping him out of his coat for the second time that day.

"Did you find her?"

He nodded. "Came right to the stable. Chaos is flighty but she's the smartest horse I've ever owned."

"Oh, good." Addy stared down at his coat. "And Coachman John is settled?"

"Coachman John is nursing a flask of whisky by a warm fire." He tugged at his sleeve. "And you might as well call me Bloodstone, or Damien—Mr. Reddington if you prefer. Don't forget, while we're here, you're Mrs. Reddington."

This was insane.

She was pretending to be the wife of a man she'd never marry but to all the world, for all she knew, she'd married him a few days ago.

The lines were more than a little blurry.

"Damien," she spoke the three syllables almost reverently. How had she come to be in a position where she had been invited to address a viscount by his given name? She certainly couldn't call him Bloodstone—*Blood*. It was far too gory-sounding to fit him.

Even if it was his family's title.

His gaze caught hers. "And you, since I obviously cannot

address you as Miss Royal, do I have permission to call you... Adelaide?"

"Of course." But only when they were alone. "I hope you don't mind that I gave our room away. I couldn't allow that poor family to sleep in the stables. Not when there was another perfectly good room. They'd have caught their death."

"It was the right thing to do." He tossed his jacket over the back of a chair. But he wasn't smiling.

"Our false names should prevent anyone here from making the connection." Addy reasoned. "I'll sleep on the floor and no one will be the wiser." She had already decided this, but Damien was shaking his head before she'd finished her sentence.

"If anyone sleeps on the floor it'll be me."

But he was a viscount. Viscounts, in Addy's mind, did not sleep on floors—especially not hard and splintered ones with questionable stains.

She wrinkled her nose.

With a decent-sized bed at their disposal, it was foolish for either of them to sleep on the floor.

"Then we'll share. We'll make a wall down the center of the bed using one of the pillows and sleep like babies knowing we've kept that poor family from having to suffer the night outside."

He raised his hand to his mouth, but nodded, a curious light in his eyes.

"Besides," she added. "Everyone thinks we're married anyway."

*A*ddy kept her thoughts to herself for at least two whole minutes, watching the viscount—*Damien*—as he took a seat and began removing his boots.

"We were lucky to get even one chamber." Her mind raced to fill in the quiet. "Did you know that the first great inns were built in centers of pilgrimages by monasteries? A large part of their business involved ale and wine, but you know that, of course. And the innkeepers posted signs using pictures instead of words to advertise to travelers." She knew she was babbling but couldn't stop herself.

She was utterly alone with a gentleman for the first time in her life.

In a room that contained a *bed!*

"Good thinking on their part." Damien said. He was kind, even if he was only humoring her. "I can't imagine many laborers knew how to read."

Little lines formed between his eyes. His hands were both elegant and strong looking as he turned his attention back to tugging the leather off his feet.

Damien, this man whom she'd be sleeping beside that night, was the perfect blend of elegance and sheer strength.

His hand slipped and he muttered a few curses under his breath.

It was almost a relief to have proof that he wasn't perfect after all.

Which brought her back to that nagging suspicion that had bothered her ever since Chloe and Captain Edgeworth's wedding.

She rolled her lips together in an attempt to keep quiet, but then burst out with: "Do you struggle with written words?"

He could read. Of course he could read. But there was something suspiciously unusual in the way he handled written documents—casually, but also as though they were about to disintegrate in his hands.

It was something she'd seen before—in a handful of her students.

He didn't answer, nor did he so much as afford her a glance as he continued tugging on the heel of his boots.

"I don't mean to be nosy. It's just that, if you do—struggle with letters—I might be able to help." She dropped onto her knees and began tugging with him, not caring that she was getting mud on her hands and the front of her gown. "And I wouldn't presume to ask if I didn't consider you a friend."

Although perhaps assuming they were friends was a presumption in itself.

Even though he'd allowed her to call him by his given name.

Damien.

The boot finally gave way, and he stilled but remained staring at the floor. "You needn't concern yourself."

"But we are friends?" she persisted.

He sighed. "Yes."

Which moved her to continue.

"Some people," Addy took hold of the opposite heel and pulled, undeterred in her mission. "For some people," she began again. "Written letters—and numbers—seem to flip around. Students have told me that they know the letters aren't really moving, but their eyes can't quite capture them. One young woman described the letters as jumping, turning backwards or upside down. Such an affliction makes reading far more difficult than it ought to be." At first Addy and Miss Primm had discussed the possibility that their vision might be impaired, but following some tests, it wasn't the case. The sensation originated somewhere between their eyes and their minds. One physician had suggested it was caused by injury, but Addy suspected most were born with the condition.

He still hadn't said a word, so Addy adjusted her hands on his heel and gave a more vigorous tug.

"Since we can't seem to cure it, we've come up with some techniques to decrease the... jumbling."

The worst part of it, she'd realized while working with such students, was that they believed themselves to be unintelligent, when in fact, they were some of the smartest to come through her classes.

The boot gave way and Lord Bloodstone, *Damien*, lifted his chin to stare up at her. Again, it struck her that she couldn't call him Bloodstone. It sounded so heartless and so... dark. The name Damien fit him perfectly. Even half covered in mud, he looked almost angelic.

One side of his mouth lifted in a half-smile. "You caught me. Most people don't notice." He exhaled and leaned back, shoeless now.

But before Addy could ask him more about his history with reading, a knock disrupted their conversation.

"I ordered a meal to be brought up." He explained, rising to answer. "The taproom wasn't all that inviting if I say so myself."

Briefly recalling the muddied floors and dirty tables, Addy readily agreed. Damien assisted her off the floor and then crossed the room in his stockinged feet.

The inn might be in somewhat of a state of filth and disrepair, but scents of an impending meal leant Addy to hope the kitchens were managed with more diligence.

"My thanks, madam." He took the tray from the maid who, although harried-looking, blossomed like a rose in spring under Damien's charm.

And then quite literally glowed when he pressed a coin into her hand.

"My name is Becca," she offered. "If you need anything at all sir, I'm happy to provide it."

Damien thanked her again, and by the time he'd closed the door behind her, that musty smell that had plagued the room had all but disappeared—overwhelmed by the aroma of freshly baked bread and some sort of savory dish.

Not having eaten since early that morning, Addy didn't dawdle but joined him at the very small table.

Digging into the meal, she pretended they'd not been interrupted.

"There are a few tricks that might help," she continued as she opened her napkin. "To make the letters jump less."

He was already breaking a piece of bread in half and

took a deliberate bite, eyeing her warily.

"If you're interested, that is." Addy pretended to be fascinated by the stew.

"You aren't going to let this go, are you?" he finally asked.

"Why would I let it go when I believe I can help you? It's just little things—nothing major." She'd seen him struggling. And she hated to watch anyone struggle.

But as he finished chewing his last bite, Addy saw his back stiffen, his countenance darkening. "Do you think that I haven't tried already?" Frustration colored his tone, though he was obviously attempting to hide it.

"What have you tried that helps?" She pretended nonchalance. One of the things she'd found helpful with her students was not to avoid discussing it. If she took a guess, she'd wager Damien had avoided the topic for most of his life.

Although her familiarity with gentlemen was limited, it was common knowledge that the male species, in general, tended to avoid discussing anything they might consider a weakness.

Addy persisted. "Newspapers are particularly tricky—with thousands of tiny characters on every page. Have you tried using a ruler to block letters on the row beneath the one you are reading? I had one student who cut out a piece of paper so that it covered the words above and below. She said there were less distractions that way—less characters flipping around the ones she was trying to read."

Damien exhaled. He acted as though he didn't care about what she had to say, but Addy could tell he was listening.

And he was thinking.

But she'd said enough.

Already, he was likely wishing her to perdition.

The first time she'd been introduced to Lord Blood-stone, she'd been in awe. And without fail, each time after that, he'd caused her heart to flutter.

She'd placed him on an imaginary pedestal, like a handsome prince reserved for some equally magnificent princess. She'd viewed him as being a person who was so perfect, so very far above her, that she could only appreciate him from a distance.

And yet here she was, sitting alone in a chamber, unchaperoned, sharing an intimate meal with him.

His golden hair appeared darker, still damp from the rain, and he had a spot of mud on one side of his face.

He was fighting to make his ale-making venture into a success. He had struggled most likely all his life when it came to reading.

He was not perfect.

She ought to have known better.

What did she even know about him? He'd lost his father or else he would not be the viscount, and she knew he had one sister whom he'd been considering sending to Miss Primm's.

And he had an abundance of friends. He was well-liked.

"What's your favorite color?" she blurted. Then she flushed, suddenly feeling like a bumbling spinster again. But she needed to be capable of light-hearted conversation if she was not to overwhelm him.

"Mine is red," she supplied. "Scarlet, actually."

He stared at her, finishing his bite. "I wouldn't have guessed that, initially."

"What color would you have guessed?" She was a little flattered that he'd contemplated her at all.

"Mint green," he said. "Something calming, soothing. But since I've come to know you a little better, I think scarlet is more appropriate."

"You no longer consider me calming?" Addy teased. Was she flirting?

She definitely was *not* flirting.

He cocked a brow. "Well, since leaving the school not quite a fortnight ago, you've scandalized me in more ways than one."

"Me? How have I done that?"

"Well, you came to my home at night without a chaperone—"

"Only because it was urgent that I speak with you about the article."

"Touché." He raised his brows but then conceded with a tilt of his head.

"How else have I scandalized you?" Addy persisted.

"With your conversation." Were those twinkles in the backs of his gorgeous eyes? "You've strayed from the weather and fashion more times than I can count. My God, woman, it's as though you like to think."

"But of course I like to think."

"Scandalous, Adelaide." He smirked. "Simply scandalous. Yes, scarlet suits you perfectly."

And to imagine she'd only picked the color because she thought it enhanced her complexion.

"What about you?" She couldn't help but grin. Even though she would never try to flirt with this viscount, this felt an awful lot like what flirting must feel like.

"Scarlet."

He appeared as surprised as she by his answer. "Because of your title?"

"No." His gaze had landed on her mouth, but then just as quickly, he went back to eating. "I don't know why."

After a not-quite-comfortable silence, Addy charged bravely forward. "And what is your favorite season?"

He finished chewing his bite before answering.

"Before my father passed, I'd have said it was winter. That man knew how to celebrate the holidays. But now... I think spring. What is yours?"

"How long ago did you lose him?"

He swallowed before answering. "About five years. The day before I turned five and twenty." He shook his head. "Your turn."

"Oh, autumn, definitely."

"Not spring? I thought all ladies preferred spring. It's the season for *The Season*, after all."

"But I'm not technically a lady," she pointed out. "Autumn is when all the students return while nature tucks itself in for the winter's rest. Just thinking about it brings up all the aromas of the leaves and cooler air..." And not wanting the conversation to lull, she asked, "What's your favorite flower?"

"Are gentlemen allowed to have a favorite flower?"

"Absolutely."

This time, he dropped his spoon into the bowl, rested his elbows on the table, and leaned forward.

She could not look away from him if her life depended on it.

"I'd have to say roses." His gaze flicked to her mouth and suddenly half the air in the room seemed to disappear. "And yours?"

***

Damien couldn't help but wonder what she tasted like. Would her pillowy lips feel as soft as they looked? Like rose petals...

"Lilacs." Her voice sounded breathy. "Not the pink or pale ones, the vibrant purple ones."

She moved on to the next question in her little game.

"Favorite food," she said.

Whereas previous conversations with Miss Adelaide Royal had been either intellectual or problem oriented, this one had taken a nonsensical turn.

It was not unpleasant.

"You must have one," she said. "Everyone does."

"Scones, fresh out of the oven. Yours is, of course—"

"Chocolate," she supplied, shaking her head. "It's one of my best memories of my mother. I remember her giving me little pieces but honestly, not much else. I remember the vanilla, the sugar, the scent of her. Nothing makes me feel better than the burst of chocolate when it melts on my tongue..." she trailed off, blushing.

His own memories washed in.

"My father loved ale," he admitted.

"Is that why—?"

"I want to make a success of the brewery." Damien needed it to be profitable. Rents hadn't been sufficient in decades. "My father began dabbling in ale before he took ill. The original recipe is his, but he only pursued it for leisure." This was a way for Damien to make the most of something he already had.

He would shore up their finances so that his mother and sister need never worry. He could solidify a legacy on the verge of collapse.

And if the brewery failed, he'd do what all titled men do.

A cold sensation trickled down his spine. His backup plan would be up in smoke if he couldn't extract himself from this situation with Adelaide—a woman who specifically did *not* have a dowry.

But also one with whom he'd struggled to resist kissing for the past ten minutes.

"You'll succeed," she said.

"From your mouth to God's ears."

But she held up her hand. "I'm not just saying it. Remember who my father is. As a child, I often traveled with him. I often did my schoolwork in his offices after school. And over the course of that time, he entertained dozens of business associates—some very successful, some not. But the successful ones, without fail, all had a certain look about them. And trust me, when you talk about your ales, you have that same look about you."

"What look?"

"Hunger—Diligence. You remind me of a lion. You see what you want, and you won't be stopped until you've succeeded." She shrugged her shoulders. "But I suppose that's just my opinion."

A decade earlier, Damien would have considered the comparison an insult. Gentlemen did not toil in trade.

But that was before.

Before he laid his father to rest.

Before he sat at his father's desk.

Before he discovered the piles of unpaid bills in the top right-hand drawer.

And Miss Adelaide Royal was not wrong. There was no way in hell he'd watch his legacy crumble. Backup plans, be damned. He'd sell more ale than anyone.

It might be his only choice.

95

WHISKEY MIGHT HAVE BEEN A MISTAKE

Several hours loomed before nightfall, so rather than sit twirling her thumbs in the chamber while Damien disappeared outside to consult with Coachman John, Addy dug out the fictional book she'd purchased on Bond Street before Chloe's wedding.

The author, a Mr. Holden Hampden, was relatively new, and his stories moved at a brisk pace as the hero explored distant lands.

That being the case, time passed swiftly, and she hardly noticed the sun lowering on the horizon before Damien returned.

He did not come empty handed.

Was he a little unsteady standing in the threshold of the open door? In one hand, he held up a deck of cards, and in the other, he dangled a half-full bottle of whisky. "Niles said they're currently out of wine."

"Niles?" Addy had been reading on the bed and pushed herself to a sitting position. Judging by the look in his now-hooded gaze, she had a good idea as to how the bottle had become half-empty.

"Niles is the innkeeper of this fine establishment." Damien stifled a hiccup and then grimaced. "My new best friend."

Addy swung her legs off the side of the bed. Her father had spent more than one late evening drinking with innkeepers.

"My father says a man who befriends servants and merchants holds more power than the president himself— or, I suppose in this case, it would be King George."

"King William now," Damien tossed the deck of cards onto the bed. And then he frowned, lost in his own thoughts. "And after the official coronation, the new queen will be Adelaide."

Addy wrinkled her nose at the reminder.

"Queen Adelaide," Damien winked, pulling the stopper out of the whisky. "Care for a splash?"

Should she? He was already half-soused. It wasn't as though she'd never tasted whisky before.

She nodded. "But don't call me that," she warned with a frown. It was just her luck that the new queen's name would be the same as hers. Another way for England to mock her.

They had hours to wait before it would be time to go to bed. Trying not to think too far into the future, Addy smoothed the counterpane where she'd been lying.

The same bed where she'd sleep that night.

Beside Damien.

Yes, whisky might be just the thing to ensure a good night's sleep.

She cleared the table where they had their meal while Damien poured the amber liquid into two short glasses.

Even from across the room, the whisky's aroma elicited a myriad of memories. Her father had also favored the spicy drink. Just as chocolate summoned memories of her mother, the whiskey reminded her of her father.

Addy pulled up a chair and began shuffling the cards while Damien set the glass in front of her. Seeing her dexterity, he flicked her a suspicious glance. "You aren't going to swindle me, are you?"

"My father would like to think I could. But no. Although I know the rules for poker and understand the best strategies, I'm terrible at bluffing."

Damien chuckled. "Of course you are."

"You'll see."

She handed the deck of cards across the table and it was his turn to impress with his shuffling.

"We don't have enough players for Whist. How about Piquet?"

"I don't know that one."

"You teach math, correct?" he asked. And at her nod, said, "You'll be a whiz at Piquet."

He removed some of the lower value cards from the deck, all the while explaining the rules. When he beat her soundly after the third hand, he leaned back and crossed one leg over the other.

"Perhaps we ought to try something else."

"Besides poker, the only other game I know is *vingt-et-un*." Probably one of the simplest games of cards to play—aside from children's games. Addy wondered what he'd say if she suggested one of the memory games the girls played during recess on raining days.

"That's as good as any." But before he flipped any cards

he took a swallow of the whisky and then leaned forward. "What are we playing for?"

A tingle of awareness reminded her of her father again. How odd it was, that a viscount exhibited traits familiar to her father.

On the surface, it was unlikely that she'd find two men who were more opposite from one another.

"Since I've nothing to wager, I'm afraid we'll have to play for bragging rights." She was not about to put up even a pence of her hard-earned money.

But Damien scowled into his glass. "No, we've got to play for something." He raised his gaze to hers and his frown stretched into a wicked grin. "Lose a hand and pay with a swallow of this rotgut."

How many had seen this side of his character? A little reckless—carefree and daring.

And fun.

Damien Reddington needed more fun in his life.

An odd thrill of anticipation settled around the table. What might he reveal about himself tonight?

"I can do that." She would play.

"I knew you wouldn't disappoint me, Adelaide Royal."

And then he winked, followed by a taunting smirk.

How was it this man could rob her of all intelligent thought with a single look?

Addy forced her attention to his hands as he dealt a single card face down for each of them. And it was impossible not to imagine his hands doing other things.

Such as holding the reins of his horse, or buttoning his jacket.

Or unfastening a lady's gown…

Feeling heat low in her belly, she blinked the image away.

"Since we're wagering drinks," he explained. "We won't wager on each card."

He peered at the card he'd dealt himself and went on to deal them both each another, this time face up.

Addy had a queen but her second was only a three. "I'll take another," she said.

A two.

"Another."

A king.

She groaned and turned over the queen.

"Drink up, Adelaide." He slid the second tumbler across the table to her.

"You can call me Addy." She lifted the glass to her nostrils for a sniff.

She'd not imbibed since she'd been in America, and even then, she'd only tasted it a few times.

It had been enough for her to learn that even the best of whisky was difficult to swallow. But none of that mattered.

She was her father's daughter, and a bet was a bet.

She tossed back her head and took it in one swallow.

"Oh!" Her eyes watered as her throat, her chest, and then her belly burned.

She was proud not to have broken into a fit of coughs.

When she'd regained her composure, she swiped at tears stinging behind her eyes. "That is quite the penalty," she said. "Are you trying to poison me?"

He didn't answer right away, but instead seemed to get lost in her gaze. "I've never known anyone like you," he finally answered and then raised his glass. "I am duly impressed."

"Let's go again." She should not feel so pleased at his approval.

The card he showed was a ten of clubs. After dealing hers, he dealt himself a five and then turned over the six.

"You're a tricky one, I see." She slid her empty glass across the table so he could pour another round.

Three more rounds and Addy's eyes stopped watering each time she drank. She could even imagine that his hands brushed hers more than necessary.

Tingling and a glance.

A lingering stroke followed by an extra beat of her heart.

Outside, the sun was mostly set, and with the flickering candles casting shadows over the perfectly chiseled lines of Damien's face, Addy imagined the two of them wrapped in a cocoon of possibility.

"You were right," he said as he dealt their fifth or sixth hand.

"Of course I was. About what?" She met his violet gaze, that vibrant color that reminded her of her favorite lilacs. The alcohol had loosened her tongue and she didn't even try to keep her thoughts to herself. "You have the most beautiful eyes I've ever seen."

"Thank you." Holding her gaze, he tapped his tongue against his top lip. "You were right about your non-existent ability to bluff." Rather than turn his attention back to their game, however, he reached across the table. "Your lip twitches right here when you're holding a winning hand." He touched the corner of her mouth.

Addy froze. What would he do if she tasted him? But before she could be so bold, he drew his hand back.

She didn't recover from his touch until he'd dealt them both new cards.

"I've never been good at dissembling," Addy forced her thoughts back to their conversation, waving one hand through the air. "I've learned to not even bother." But then she pointed a finger at him. "You, on the other hand, are a devil when it comes to hiding your emotions.

He flipped her next card and then filled her glass again.

"And not only while playing cards," she continued.

Liquid courage filled her with confidence she didn't normally possess.

Or did that confidence come from basking in his attention for the past few hours?

"You hide whatever you are really thinking with charm. You smile and bow and compliment people, but deep inside, you're hiding your true thoughts."

"Think you're pretty smart, do you?"

"I'm smarter than I look," Addy answered.

The rain had mostly subsided to a constant drizzle but in that moment, thunder rumbled in the distance.

"Smart and pretty," he said. "You have the most beautiful mouth I've ever laid eyes on."

His words sent a shiver through her. It was possible he was simply mocking the compliment she'd given him, but she couldn't be sure.

"Case in point," she said. "You're changing the subject by turning the same compliment back on me."

"Not the same. I refer to your mouth, whereas you complimented my eyes."

"But you used the word beautiful, the same as I did."

"Luscious, then." He leaned forward.

Addy folded her arms along the table and leaned in as well.

If he was going to do better, than so was she. "Your eyes are dreamy. Dreamy and unfathomable."

"Succulent. Sweet," he said.

"Deep. Mysterious."

"Kissable."

Any air she'd managed to keep in her lungs swooshed away. "Have you kissed many women, then?"

"Enough. And I know kissable lips when I see them."

His gaze flicked to her mouth and then back to her eyes.

"You could be wrong."

"I'm not," he rejoined immediately.

How did one respond to such a boast?

Butterflies swarmed her insides and she pressed herself forward another inch.

How had they gone from discussing bluffing at card games to contemplating how kissable his mouth was?

Not *his* mouth, she corrected her pronoun. *Her* mouth.

Although she'd be lying to herself if she didn't admit she'd wondered about his.

Firm. Soft but also strong.

Irresistible.

But then his gaze dropped from hers and he flipped his card over. "Twenty-one."

How could he flip back to the cards so easily?

Addy exhaled. Men such as Damien Reddington, a viscount, no less, did not go about kissing bluestocking schoolteachers.

Even if they were reportedly married to them.

***

The whisky had been a mistake. Damien had no business

thinking about kissing this woman. Or doing any of the other things his mind conjured up.

Then again, he may be going to have to marry her anyway.

The fact that such a thought didn't turn his veins to ice could only be attributed to the whisky.

Which was, indeed, a mistake.

Having worked their way through the deck of cards, he watched as she methodically turned every single card face down across the table while explaining the rules of her memory game.

Something he remembered from when he was a child. The concept was almost too simple.

And yet he found himself playing her game, turning cards over, remembering where he'd found what, and putting together matches.

Each time one of them found a match, the other took a swallow of whisky. When they ran out of whisky, they switched to water.

The sky outside the window had long since faded from greyish blue to black.

But inside, where the candles burned down to their nubs, the two of them barely noticed.

Because while playing every card game they could possibly come up with, he and this woman—who was not his wife—shared childhood stories, a few fears, and also a few dreams.

She'd been raised mostly by her father, was afraid of being alone, and dreamt of one day running her own school.

Because she'd never have a family of her own.

He told her stories about his younger sister, that he

feared having to sell off parts of his estate, and dreamt of brewing the perfect ale, which he no doubt described to her in far too much detail.

It was the most unusual, and yet one of the most enjoyable, evenings he'd experienced in a very long time.

So enjoyable, in fact, that he needed to put an end to it.

"You can change behind the screen." He almost took her by the hand and led her to the bed instead. It would have felt natural.

But they had not crossed a certain line. Despite that he liked her.

He liked her very much.

But he needed to be rational.

If necessary, he'd do the honorable thing, but until then, he wasn't prepared to relinquish the security of knowing he could marry a woman who came with a decent-sized dowry.

"I'm so tired I can hardly raise my arms." Adelaide's voice drifted to him from where she was changing.

Good God, but all of this was improper.

You're going to have to marry her anyway. His conscience taunted him. *Dowry or not.*

Damien climbed onto the very soft mattress fully clothed but for his waistcoat and jacket. After a moment's thought, he removed the pillow from behind his head and placed it in a spot where it would be between them.

And then he feigned sleep.

A BIT OF A QUANDARY

*A*ddy went to roll away from the warmth beside her only to discover that she was trapped. Was she dreaming? No, she'd slept like the dead. So why, then, was she not alone?

She opened her eyes but saw only darkness. It was his scent that brought the night back to her.

Her thoughts drifted to the card games, the whisky, the easy conversation interjected with unusual moments of a charged sort of awareness.

In those moments she'd believed he might kiss her, but he had not.

After she'd changed into her night rail, she'd found him already asleep, all but clinging to his side of the bed.

And...

She'd been disappointed.

Her disappointment came only because a most pleasant evening had come to an end. It had nothing to do with her unkissed state.

If not for the table between them, there had been at least

three particular instances where she'd caught him staring at her mouth, where she'd been sure he was going to lean forward and touch his lips to hers.

Had that been her imagination? Had she conjured those tension-filled moments from wishful thoughts helped along by the intimacy of their situation and a quarter bottle of rotgut whisky?

He had not kissed her.

She'd not gone to bed right away but restlessly moved around the room, extinguishing candles before climbing into the opposite side of the bed.

And yet despite commendable attempts on both their parts to sleep on their designated halves of the bed, at some time during the night, they'd both rolled into the middle.

Gravity.

It was like that.

That was the only likely explanation as to how Adelaide Elizabeth Royal found herself sleeping in Viscount Bloodstone's arms.

Damien.

The name of an angel.

She felt warm, and safe, and perhaps more protected than she'd felt in a very long time. If she had a home, she'd want it to feel like this.

"Um…" His voice hummed sleepily, and he tightened his arm around her.

And then his mouth landed on the back of her neck, warm and wet, sending hot sensations coursing her into an acute wakefulness.

Was he awake?

Did he even know what he was doing?

"I see the pillow wasn't an effective barrier after all," his voice broke into her thoughts, answering her questions before she could wrestle with them.

"Apparently not," she answered and then held her breath.

If he was awake, it meant he had consciously placed his lips against the back of her neck.

And when he awoke, he had not shoved her away from him.

The hand even now stroking her arm was doing so intentionally.

"Hell of a quandary we've gotten ourselves into, Adelaide."

Which quandary was he referring to? The announcement in the Gazette? The fact that they'd gotten themselves caught in a rainstorm?

Or the fact that his body was pressed against hers, and even as she lie here, her heart raced in anticipation of a million different possibilities.

And if she concentrated very hard, she felt his heart racing too.

Along with other…

Things.

"It is," she agreed, and then caught her breath when his lips trailed around her neck—nuzzling the sensitive skin just along her hairline.

"I promised myself I wouldn't kiss you." His breath fanned her flesh.

"Oh." Brilliant, Adelaide. *Oh?* "Why?"

He chuckled at her questions. At her? Or was he laughing at himself?

But she didn't really need his answer to know why.

He'd wish to maintain proprieties. Proprieties that had

flown out the window the minute he'd stepped inside this chamber.

That was when time stopped and all of this turned unreal. Their time together had become a timeout from reality—an interlude that didn't count.

An interlude that could never amount to anything more than a memory.

A dream.

Last night had been an evening where neither of them had conformed to the people society expected them to be. They had simply been Damien and Adelaide.

A man and a woman.

And the sun had yet to rise on a new day.

Damien's mouth had progressed to her shoulder while his hand trailed around to splay over her belly, just beneath her breasts.

"I wanted you to kiss me," she admitted.

His mouth grazed her jaw now, stubbles of whiskers awakening her sensitive skin.

"I know." His voice was almost a growl.

Of course he knew. Because, as she'd told him, she'd never been any good at bluffing.

And she hadn't only wanted him to kiss her, she'd craved for him to kiss her. She'd *ached* for it.

She closed her eyes and inhaled his scent. Whisky and spice—not quite cinnamon—ginger and bergamot.

"Damien." She twisted in his arms and raised her face to his.

His taste was not unlike his scent, but it was richer—raw and masculine.

Him. She'd never forget this taste.

"What are we doing?" His mouth left hers just long enough to breathe.

But then he was tasting her and she was tasting him. His tongue explored along her teeth while he inhaled her breath.

Adelaide had been kissed before, but nothing like this. A swell of something hard pressed against her belly and she'd never felt such a sense of... rightness. She'd never known such an all-encompassing desire to surrender her entire being.

Madness stirred inside her. *This isn't real*, she reminded herself even as he hooked her knee around his hip.

"So good," he murmured against her skin. He'd abandoned her lips to meander lower.

Wet heat on her breast, tugging, pinching.

"So good," she echoed. She wanted him to know she was willing, that she was curious and open and wanting. She clutched her arms around his back, arching into him, trying to feed the aching between her legs.

Harsh breathing echoed in her ears, and she was startled to realize it was hers. "Damien," she moaned.

He shifted, then, turning so he was above her.

In all their twisting and touching, her gown was around her waist and Damien was nestled between her thighs. He raised himself up, fumbling with the fasteners on his falls and...

The mattress whooshed out from beneath her, followed by a loud, jarring thump.

For a full thirty seconds, neither Adelaide nor Damien either moved or spoke.

And in the space of that time, the aching need managed to protest and subside at the same time.

It was as though the universe would make one last gasp to prevent them from taking this step—from locking themselves into a lifetime by giving in to one night of physical longing.

When Damien's head fell forward, limp and remorseful, Adelaide could almost read his thoughts.

"I'm sorry," she said by rote of habit. Because all of this was her fault.

She never should have insisted that Chloe have a bouquet for her wedding.

When Chloe refused the flowers, Addy never should have kept them for herself.

And most of all, she should never have given into the stupid impulse to toss those flowers. He never would have thrown the coin if she hadn't.

"No. It's my fault." But he still hadn't and she was acutely aware of his member pressing against her thigh.

He still wanted her. Evidence of a struggle between his body and mind flickered in his expression.

So she wiggled and then pushed at his shoulders. "We can't."

"I know." In one graceful motion, he rolled off her, leaving both of them lying on their backs, staring up into the darkness.

Addy tugged her night rail back down to cover herself. Not that he could see anything, but to put one thin layer of separation between them.

Even if she didn't want it.

Did she?

Her heart squeezed even tighter when he sat up and swung his feet off the edge of the mattress.

Which now rested at an awkward angle on the floor.

"I suppose we ought to be grateful for Nile's shoddy maintenance."

"I suppose," Addy said. Because there was some part deep inside of her that wondered if it all would be for naught anyway.

Because there was no way of knowing who'd taken note of that fallacious announcement this week.

And the likelihood that they'd come out of this unscathed seemed more unlikely with every hour.

SO MUCH FOR THE BACKUP PLAN

*D*amien closed the door behind him as he stepped into the darkness beneath the covered porch. The unmistakable aroma of mud and manure filled the air. Only a few dripping sounds remained from the heavy rain.

He supposed he ought to be grateful that the storm had passed.

There was no way he could remain in that bed, or in that chamber for that matter, without doing something that would lock both of them into this forever.

Blast and damn.

He'd already compromised her.

Perhaps he hadn't ruined her in the eyes of society, nor had he taken the final step of robbing her of her innocence, but he might as well have.

And it didn't matter that she wasn't some Mayfair debutante. She could be a chamber maid, by God, and his conscience would nag at him after what he'd just very nearly done.

The sky gradually lightened in the east while he paced

back and forth along the raised wooden porch that extended the length of the inn. If not for the mud, he could have gone for a run—done something that required more exertion to work off this uncomfortable feeling of unsatisfied lust and undeterred guilt.

Damned bed.

Would he have gone through with it?

He summoned the feel of her soft form beneath him, open, and more than willing, and his erection, which had finally relaxed to half-mast, surged back to life.

Even the cool morning air failed to cool the blood racing through his veins.

He would have gone through with it.

Hell, everyone thought they were married anyway.

But once he'd stopped, she'd agreed it was a mistake. In fact, she'd pushed him away.

Damien clenched his hands together, and then ran a hand through his hair.

The world was going to believe they were married regardless. He was a fool to think otherwise.

His pacing turned into an angry march, and the urge to jump out of his skin made him itch all over.

Their fate had been sealed the day she'd barged into his study carrying that damn newspaper.

He wasn't ready for this.

He wasn't ready to relinquish his backup plan.

Blast and damn. Mud or not, he took off running down the road and cursed, but was not deterred, when the first drops of rain landed on his face.

The storm, apparently, hadn't subsided after all.

***

Addy didn't even try going back to sleep.

After lighting the candles around the room, she'd washed and then dressed and located one of the maids already toiling downstairs in the kitchen.

Damien was nowhere in sight. She could only presume he'd gone out to the stables.

By the time the sun made its appearance, a tray of chocolate and biscuits had been delivered to her chamber, and a temporary repair had been made so the bed no longer slanted on the floor.

Leaving Addy with nothing to do but sit and read—or try, anyway.

She'd read the same page at least five times and had no idea what the protagonist had accomplished.

Where was Damien?

He could not have gone far. Perhaps he had made a bed on some bale of hay—anything to get away from her.

Was he angry?

Sorry?

Was he as frustrated as she was?

Because if he was, it portended another troublesome night.

They couldn't travel today. Even though the rain had become sporadic, the muddied roads would be impassable. And since no one else could travel, there would be no opportunity to take a second chamber.

Their current predicament tumbled around in her brain in addition to concerns over what Miss Primm was going to say. She determined she'd make one more attempt to read her book when someone knocked on the door.

"Who is there?"

"It's me."

Was he knocking? On his own chamber door?

Addy swallowed an unrecognizable emotion before calling out. "Come in."

Setting her book aside, she rose while self-consciously touching the knot she'd pinned at the back of her head.

She wasn't prepared for the sight that met her, and if she hadn't heard his voice, might not have recognized the man standing in the threshold.

He was soaked from head to toe. Her eyes trailed down, noticing that he must have had to leave his boots outside and wore only stockings on his feet. Streaks and globs of mud caked onto his breeches, with a few splatters on his shirt, and a few even on his face.

"What—?" she shook her head.

"I went for a run." He shrugged as though running through muck at dawn was a natural occurrence. And then he glanced around the room. "You've been busy. Is that tea?"

"Chocolate," she answered, choosing to ignore his bedraggled state for now. "You must be ready to break your fast. Do you often go for morning runs?" She moved back to the chair where she'd been sitting.

"Whenever I can." But then he dropped his shoulders and pinned his gaze on hers. "We need to talk."

Addy's gut clenched. She'd half expected this. Was he going to depart alone on his horse? It would be dangerous for both him and his mount, but perhaps he considered his association with her even more of a threat.

To his bachelorhood.

To his estate.

To his future.

"Yes," she agreed and leaning forward, poured him a cup of the steaming liquid. Normally the scent of chocolate calmed her, but even the sweet vanilla flavors wafting from the pot failed to keep her heart from faltering.

"You needn't worry about me." She would head off the sting of rejection. "Even if Primm lets me go, I'm not without means. I simply need to locate my father and I'll be fine."

If her father handed over some of her dowry, she could invest in a school somewhere. If her reputation was stained beyond repair, she could always return to America.

But her heart weighed heavy to imagine having to do either.

The school was the only place she'd felt at home since coming to England.

You feel at home with Damien.

You felt at home in his arms.

She ignored the fanciful reminders.

Damien pulled out the opposite chair, the same one he'd sat in the night before while they'd finished off the whisky, but this time they were drinking the chocolate.

"What do you want, Adelaide?"

"What do you mean?" His question wasn't at all what she'd expected.

"What do *you* want for yourself—for Adelaide Royal?"

Oh, but this wasn't fair.

"Does it matter what I want?" In most of the course of her adult life, her wants were so far down the list of priorities as to never have been taken into consideration.

"Of course it matters." He tilted his head. "Why wouldn't it matter?"

"And I thought I was naïve." She smiled to soften her statement and kept going before he could contradict her. "I know what you want. You want to make a success of your brewery to strengthen the financial state of your legacy. But if your endeavor fails, you'll have to marry well. Perhaps you'll want to marry well anyhow—which isn't a bad idea as it's always good to keep reserves on hand."

He'd leaned back in his chair and by the end of her rambling, had returned his cup of chocolate to the table and folded his arms over his chest.

"You are partially right," he said when she was through. "But also partially wrong. My life consists of more than a ledger of debits and credits." At this point he frowned. "I'm not your father."

"Of course you're not my father!" It was a horrifying thought. "I didn't mean to imply that you were mercenary. It's just that—"

"There is such a matter as honor." He shifted in his chair. "I—"

"But we don't know if there are any public ramifications of the announcement yet. Or of…" She gestured around the room. "Any of this. And until we do, we absolutely should not make any decisions."

Damien dropped his hands and leaned forward. "I'm not talking about public opinion. I'm talking about…" He gestured toward the bed. "It doesn't matter that you're a schoolteacher from America or the daughter of a duke, a gentleman who claims to uphold his honor doesn't…"

"What?" she asked, noting his lowered brows and the hard line of his jaw.

He shook his head. "I have to marry you."

ANOTHER NIGHT TOGETHER

"No!" Adelaide burst out of her chair. Not that the prospect of marrying such an honorable and handsome gentleman didn't tempt her on some very basic level, but not like this...

Not as some sort of punishment to him for doing nothing more than ensuring she made it safely back to the school.

And for securing a chamber for them in the face of inclement weather.

And for...

Snuggling her.

Most certainly not to remedy an erroneous announcement made by an incompetent reporter.

"You need to marry someone with a dowry!" she added as she paced to the opposite side of the room. Without a dowry to bring into a marriage, she'd be nothing more than a burden.

And whenever he experienced any sort of financial distress, he'd have her to blame.

"I thought you said I was a lion." He was smiling.

Smiling!

She hated when people threw her own words back in her face. "You are, but—"

"Does this mean you don't genuinely believe I'm going to profit handsomely off the sale of my ale?"

Addy halted her pacing and blinked at him. "You'll succeed," she said. "I'm ninety-nine percent sure of that. But if you don't, you need your backup plan."

Now he was laughing outright.

"Adelaide. You are one of a kind, you know that?"

But Addy wasn't laughing. She hugged her arms at her waist. "It's too drastic. We need to wait," she said.

He sobered up and stared at her. "It's doubtful we're going to extract ourselves from this." Again, he gestured around the room. "Any of it. I didn't think this through…"

"It's not the innkeeper and his guests that I'm worried about. They think we're married regardless." It was Miss Primm. And all the other teachers. And her students' parents.

And his mother. And his mother's friends. And all of society.

And then there was always her aunt.

And her father.

Damien exhaled and ran a hand through his hair. He grimaced when he stared at his hand. Mud.

"Very well."

Addy glanced toward the door. "I'll request a bath for you—and make myself scarce, of course. And after we've spoken with Miss Primm we can revisit this discussion." She frowned and added, "If necessary."

Perhaps she'd look in on Coachman John. Or offer her

assistance in the kitchens. Whatever she did, she'd make certain to stay as far from their chamber as possible while he cleaned up.

Even if a part of her contemplated that he was without a valet and might need some assistance.

While sitting naked in a tub of soapy water.

Adelaide forced herself to ignore the devilish voice whispering in her ear. *Why don't you wash his back? Who will pour the pitcher of water over his head?*

Conjured images of bubbles of soap sliding down slick sinewy shoulders and chest had her shuffling toward the door.

What was wrong with her?

Whatever it was, she was going to have to get it under control. Because they had at least one more night alone in this chamber and at the rate she was going, she might not push him away the next time she found herself lying beneath him.

***

The woman was going to be the death of him.

Twenty minutes after Adelaide bolted from their chamber, three stout employees arrived with a rusty tub and heated water.

A bath would make him feel human again. Determined to dismiss Adelaide Royal from his thoughts, he climbed into the tub and did his level best to scrub the morning away.

Had she seriously declined his proposal? By God, she had.

Adelaide might initially appear compliant and agreeable,

but when push came to shove, she was as contrary as his mother's cat.

Bending his knees, he leaned back and ducked his head under the water. The tub might be old, but it was large and the water was hot and mostly clean.

He ought to have allowed her first crack at it.

She wasn't caked in mud like him but she would no doubt have appreciated a hot soak.

And now there was a vision he ought not to have summoned.

He imagined her reddish-blond hair pinned up, with damp strands clinging to her neck. Her shoulders would be that creamy color, untouched, rounded and feminine. Hints of her bosom would peek over the edge of the tub as she slid the wet cloth over her skin.

He moved his hand to his cock and he contemplated the wisdom, but also the necessity, of a satisfying release.

True, she could return any minute, possibly interrupting him and leaving him to recover yet again. But judging by the look on her face when she'd exited, he doubted she'd be back for a few hours.

Furthermore, he had another night to spend with her alone. Sharing a bed.

With her tucked against him in nothing more than a thin night rail.

Damien worked his hand along his shaft, remembering the taste of her skin as he'd buried his face between her breasts—how the tips had tightened into firm little buds, the perfect shape and size for his mouth.

And how she'd writhed against him, wrapping her legs around his waist.

He increased the pace of his fist, as well as the pressure.

She'd be tight and wet. Velvety flesh would pulse around him.

And she'd make those little sounds in her throat—sounds of pleasure and excitement she'd been helpless to keep to herself.

Energy pulsed through his core, and with three more strokes, painful satisfaction surged down his spine.

Damien hissed through his teeth, and allowed relief to roll through him.

ONLY A KISS

*A*ddy spent as much time away as she could before returning to their chamber, waiting to go up until ten minutes after she watched the tub be carried back down the stairs.

Interrupting his bath was not something for which she was prepared to add to her list of social transgressions.

And when she arrived outside their chamber door, she shifted the tray of food she'd procured onto one hand and knocked softly.

"Damien?"

No response.

Had he slipped back outside when she wasn't looking?

Three more knocks. "Damien?"

When he still didn't answer, she pushed the door open and then halted.

Barefoot, wearing only a wrinkled white linen shirt tucked into a clean pair of breeches, Damien lay on his side in the center of the bed, sound asleep.

She closed the door behind her and tiptoed inside.

Crisp strands of his golden hair shot up in all directions, and his hands were tucked against his face.

For an instant, she could imagine him as he must have appeared as a child.

But he was no boy.

As a viscount, as a man, regardless of what he was doing, he possessed a natural air of authority.

And in sleep…

He was simply…

Beautiful.

She lowered the tray onto the small table and then crept closer to the bed, unable to drag her gaze away from his sleeping form.

Her hands itched to brush his hair away from his face—to trace a line down his chest…

Not falling for this man might be the most difficult task ever laid out for one woman.

She clenched her hands together.

This isn't real, she reminded herself. They were not a married couple stranded on the way to his home. They had been forced into one another's proximity in another universe—in a false reality.

She was not really Mrs. Reddington, just as she was not the Viscount of Bloodstone.

She was Miss Royal—math and science teacher at Miss Primm's—daughter of the Mad American Royal.

Cold settled in her veins and she turned away from the bed. Addy located her book and got as comfortable as she could on one of the wooden chairs.

She would read and allow him to sleep.

And although it took her three times to drag her gaze across the same page, she eventually lost herself in the adventures of Bartholomew Brown, an adventurous Englishman at war with pirates who'd stolen the treasure he'd found on a tropical island.

A treasure which he intended to donate to a struggling London orphanage owned by Sylvia Sweetbottom.

"Are you reading the latest mathematical theories? Or the newest scientific discoveries?" Damien's voice pulled her out of the story from across the room.

"You're awake," she jumped guiltily. "I would have left you alone but the taproom was already filling up and—"

"No. I'm glad you've returned. Not all of good old Niles' guests possess gentlemanly manners."

"Precisely." But then Addy lifted the book. "And this is neither math nor science, but fiction. Holden Hampden, have you heard of him?" She was sensitive to Damien's challenges where reading was concerned but she would not assume he avoided it altogether.

His answer was something of a grimace.

And seeing him looking so… unmasked as he sat on the edge of the bed, her heart swelled.

"What kind of stories?" He ran a hand down his face.

"Travels, mostly. Reminds me of Robinson Crusoe but with romantic elements that for me, anyhow, make the story more entertaining."

Damien's gaze flicked to the table and she added, "I brought up some bread, cheese, and meats earlier. There is some fruit too if you're interested."

She knew she was babbling but couldn't stop herself, that was, until his violet stare locked onto hers.

All morning she'd convinced herself she could pretend nothing had happened between the two of them. She could pretend he'd not had his mouth on hers, and… other places.

She could pretend she hadn't tasted the essence of his desire.

But looking into his eyes…

"You've been busy," he shifted his gaze back to the table. "While I've slept the day away."

"Neither of us got much sleep last night. I imagine running in the rain wears a person out."

He looked like he might add to that but then sighed and crossed to the table. "Don't stop reading on my account." He lifted one of the covers off the food and then tore off a piece of bread.

"I'm at a rather interesting part. Captain Nutter's ship— he's the villain—is under siege, and the hero, Bartholomew Brown, is chained belowdecks in the hull."

"I'm all ears." Damien half-grinned. "If you don't mind reading aloud. What else is there to do?" Whereas all sorts of inappropriate ideas recklessly jumped into Addy's thoughts, she tamped down on her fluttering heart while he calmly cut off a slice of the cheese and folded it between his bread.

"You want me to…? Of course." Addy cleared her throat. The story was inherent with certain ribald references and wasn't exactly meant to be read in mixed company. Luckily, this section was a safe one.

And for the next half an hour, Addy lost herself again, reading to a half-dressed viscount while he enjoyed a midday meal.

Bartholomew Brown had found himself in dire straits.

"Explosions boomed from above, inciting a bevy of terrified screams from fellows at the opposite end of the chain. Until that moment, I had never been concerned at the prospect of meeting my maker, but I considered it then. Alas, though. I refused to believe

my time had come. Sylvia Sweetbottom needed saving and I was all she had."

Addy's gaze rushed to the next paragraph which went on to describe the battle threatening to put an end to Bartholomew's existence. By the time she'd finished the chapter, Damien had reclined on the opposite chair, one ankle resting on his knees, watching her and looking amused.

"Entertaining fellow, that Holden Hampden." And then he stared unfocused at the near-empty tray on the table. "What sort of... tricks did you and your students come up with?"

Tricks? Addy frowned, confused. What exactly was he asking?

But then the meaning of his question struck her and she had to stifle her excitement.

"Let me show you." She cleared a spot on the table and then moved her chair so that she could sit beside him. Annoyed to see her hands shaking, she picked up one of the napkins and folded it in half making a straight edge. "It's easier with foolscap, but you get the idea," she explained.

Keeping the book pinched open, she set her little contraption directly in front of him. "Have you tried this before?"

He shook his head but kept his attention on how she was using the napkin. The fact that he had suffered from word blindness his entire life but still managed to learn to read was an impressive feat. And he hadn't only learned to read, but he'd learned the ins and outs of managing his estate.

Had he ever given himself credit for that?

"Eliminating unnecessary letters allows you to focus on the ones you want to read." When writing out instructions for her students, she used bullet points and short lists. She printed in large clear letters and removed time constraints if possible.

Unfortunately, there would always be circumstances where these issues were out of her students' control.

Or in this case, the viscount's.

She explained a few other tricks while he placed the napkin as she instructed.

When she leaned in to straighten the edge, their arms touched from shoulder to wrist causing her breath to hitch.

"Some students cut rectangular holes in the paper so it covers the line over and under..." Her bodice felt tighter than it had earlier.

How was she expected to think rationally when his proximity was all it took to rob her of her equilibrium?

"If you trust your valet, or butler, or have some reliable associate, you might ask them to print out documents that aren't written in script—such as—"

"A marriage certificate." He shot her a self-deprecating grimace.

"But you made your way through it." Addy wanted to praise him for his accomplishments but sensed it would only embarrass him.

"I had no choice," Damien said. "The other witness was waiting impatiently to have her chance at it." He turned to face her, their faces less than a foot apart. "Did you know then?"

"I suspected."

He licked his lips and then turned to her. "So I'm lucky enough to be traveling with a tutor. One who's more than willing to advise a viscount."

"I'm happy to help."

"That's good to know."

His gaze dropped to her mouth.

Was his breathing as shallow as hers?

And then he leaned forward, cutting those twelve inches in half. "I shouldn't, but I want to kiss you again."

"You do?" Oh, but she wanted it too.

"But I shouldn't."

"Right," she breathed, her mouth aching to taste his. It was as though a magnet was drawing her closer to him, one which got harder and harder to resist with each passing second. "But it doesn't have to mean anything. It's not as though it will change anything. Everyone thinks we're married anyway."

"True." But the sound wasn't as optimistic as she hoped.

And yet he gathered her in his arms and eliminated the final six inches separating them.

This kiss was very different from the embrace they'd shared on the bed. This one was tentative, cautious.

Addy remained in her chair and Damien in his.

Each flick of the tongue asked for another. Each inhaled breath granted it.

"Kissing won't change anything," Addy repeated.

Damien's hands cradled her face now, and he turned his head to improve their connection. "Won't it?"

With better access, his tongue swept inside, grazing the top of her mouth, the softer sides, and then smoothing along her teeth.

And Addy reciprocated, teasing inside his, drinking in his taste and the delightful foreign sensations of just—

Of just kissing.

The kiss could have lasted ten seconds or ten minutes.

She lost all track of time and when their mouths reluctantly separated, both were breathing heavily.

Damien tasted better than she could have possibly guessed. Better, even, than chocolate. Addy wanted more.

Damien pulled her across the space between them, adjusting her on his lap.

"Schoolteachers," he exhaled almost to himself. "No wonder Hardwood and Edgeworth were caught so easily," Damien chuckled beneath his breath.

But his words pricked something in her head and she leaned back. "Caught?"

"Caught in marriage traps." Damien spoke as though he was teasing. But Addy blinked.

"There were no marriage traps." She defended Chloe and Priscilla.

"No, the woman themselves were the marriage traps." A line appeared between his eyes—eyes which appeared slightly concerned at this point—concerned no doubt at the tension that had taken hold of her.

"Women are *not* traps," she said.

Damien scowled. "It's just that a few of the teachers from Miss Primm's, women of intelligence, were not inclined to bow to the stricter rules of society."

"You mean that we are... wanton?"

"I'm merely suggesting that they think for themselves."

"But you implied that my friends acted without virtue so that they could trap the captain and the earl." She pushed herself off his lap.

Did he imagine she was doing the same? Did he believe she'd set out to trap him thusly?

She had agreed to his escort. "Did you think that's what I

was doing when I gave up the second chamber? Trying to trap you?"

Damien blinked and jerked his head back.

"But you did that out of the goodness of your heart. You had no ulterior motive." And then his gaze narrowed. "Or did you?"

"Oh!" Addy's hands fisted at her sides. "Of course not! If you remember correctly, it was you who escorted me out of the church! It was you who insisted on riding in the same hackney with me! And might I remind you of the coins?"

With his kiss still burning on her lips, she began scooping up the dishes and gathered up the tray.

"Where are you going?"

"I'm taking this downstairs to the kitchen." She sniffed. "If you're finished, that is."

"Oh, I'm finished." He was out of his seat now and paced across to the window. "With any luck we can leave this Godforsaken inn first thing tomorrow morning."

"Harumph." Addy didn't know what else to say so she marched into the corridor and closed the door firmly behind her.

It wasn't until she'd delivered the tray and marched outside that she wondered what had just happened between them.

FALLING

*A*delaide Royal had picked a fight with him.

In the middle of a thoroughly satisfying kiss, she'd gone and picked a fight.

Had what he said really been all that insulting? Damien had considered it something of a compliment at the time.

Irritated by her irrational behavior, he paced across to the small hearth and scrubbed one hand through his hair.

Women!

She'd had been the one to insist that kissing wouldn't change anything.

He's the one who ought to have picked a fight.

He lowered himself to the chair and wrestled one foot into his boot.

His *ruined* boot, that was, with the leather stiff from the water and mud crusted along the laces. *Blast and damn.* Everything was ruined!

He could pretend all he liked, but deep down he knew he was going to have to marry her.

Oh, but wait, she'd already told him no.

If that was what she wanted, it was fine with him!

Reaching to loosen his cravat, his hands fumbled when they landed on nothing but the top buttons of his shirt. This was going to drive him insane.

Was this to be the end of his bachelorhood? With the room closing in around him, Damien struggled into his jacket.

There were three things a gentleman could do while stranded in an inn due to inclement weather: Drink, swive, and gamble, and not necessarily in that order.

Well, he'd already done the first. And the second was out of the question. Perhaps Niles knew of a real game of cards —one where they played for coin, not swallows of rotgut.

He glanced around and his gaze landed on Adelaide's book, the napkin she'd folded, and her night rail draped over the screen.

He needed out of this ramshackle of a room. Away from the constant reminders of that damned announcement.

Away from the bed where he'd very nearly taken her innocence.

Would he have her tonight?

He ignored the thought and stormed into the foyer. Feeling less than gracious considering the turn his future was taking, he then slammed the door behind him and marched downstairs to the tap room.

Where, in this frame of mind, he was certain to fit in with all the other ungentlemanly fellows.

***

Adelaide released the wooden post and stepped off the long wooden porch onto the ground. The rain had stopped coming down and she thought she spied a hint of blue on the horizon.

Even so, her half boot sunk a few inches into the mud.

But she'd been shooed out of the kitchens. The only place she could go was back up to the room.

The room she shared with *that... man!*

How dare he suggest her friends had trapped his? All three of her friends who'd married had fallen in love and become engaged with their prospective spouses in an organic manner.

She was one hundred percent sure.

Well, ninety-nine percent sure.

Maneuvering to a grassy patch, Addy walked in the opposite direction of wafting manure.

He'd said they trapped them, hadn't he? No, he'd said the women themselves were the traps—objects of temptation.

She *fumed.*

Her friends were not responsible for his friends' feelings! How dare he suggest such a horrid notion!

He'd accused them of being... *"women of intelligence"* who weren't *"inclined to succumb to the stricter rules of society."*

Addy frowned. He wasn't the first man to speak of women in such a demeaning way. The notion was a rampant one and...

Despite the cold mud and water seeping into her boots, her blood boiled. Men must be responsible for their own actions!

Idiots. All of them. She increased her pace. *Seething.*

No wonder Chloe had conceded to marriage so reluctantly. It meant she would tie herself to one of...

Them!

Damien had accused them of being wanton. Hadn't he?

135

She scrunched her nose.

No, she'd said that.

"I'm merely suggesting that they think for themselves," he'd said. Had that been an accusation?

As far as insults go, it wasn't all that bad, really. In fact, Chloe, no doubt, might even consider it a compliment.

As would Victoria and possibly even Priscilla.

"Women of intelligence" who weren't *"inclined to succumb to the stricter rules of society."*

But he'd insulted them, hadn't he?

Addy bit her lip. She had been the one to imply that he thought they'd acted without virtue.

Her steps slowed.

And he had also defended her decision to give up the second room.

Even so...

She summoned a surge of her anger. After defending her, he had agreed that she might have had untoward intentions when giving up their second chamber—that she'd *wanted* to share a single chamber with him...

Sort of.

A cool breeze shook the leaves above, sending mists of water into the air.

Addy shivered and then hugged her arms in front of her.

Had the argument been partially her fault?

Did she owe him an apology?

He'd been kissing her so nicely. Heat had flooded her core and she'd felt his arousal.

"Schoolteachers. No wonder both Hardwood and Edgeworth were caught so easily."

More effectively than a bucket of cold water, his words had shocked her back to reality.

She had been on the verge of giving him her innocence and he'd lumped her in with schoolteachers in general.

His implication had been that there was nothing original about her as an individual, consequentially painting her as unworthy.

Hadn't he?

In her fuming and ruminations Addy had marched up a hill, which, although not overly steep, afforded a view for miles around. In the distance, she could make out slim streams of smoke coming from the inn's chimneys.

She needed to return and apologize. His words had come out insensitive but she would accept partial blame for their argument.

Having decided to return to their chamber and negotiate a truce, she spun around to turn back. The ground, unfortunately, wasn't inclined to allow her departure.

In place where she'd been standing, the dirt shifted and then slipped away from the hill.

With nothing to grab, her arms flailed and gravity took over, sending her tumbling head over heels.

And almost as though it was happening to someone else, Addy watched as the clouds tumbled past her, and then the grass and trees and then the clouds again, and more trees.

As a child, she'd occasionally entertained herself by rolling down one of the hills on her father's estate. But she'd scouted out the terrain beforehand, crossed her arms in front of her, and been generally prepared for such an adventure.

Grown now, and without warning, the experience was more vexing than entertaining. And at some point, she felt like she'd lost her stomach. Tree roots and prickly plants, rather than soft grass, made up most of the terrain.

But the worst of it, by far, was that she had no assurances that she wouldn't slam into anything, nor that she'd stop at all.

Anything could be awaiting her at the bottom: a lake, a stream, a wall of rocks...

An unexpected cliff.

Her life flashed before her eyes and her rolling slowed. When she came to a complete stop, she simply lay staring up at the sky, watching two birds flutter over her as the wind pushed the clouds slowly toward the west.

It was the damp seeping through her gown that eventually stirred her to action. She'd lived, of course, she'd lived, but was she breathing?

She rolled onto her side, gasping a little, and when she went to push herself up, winced at the stinging in her hands. When she did manage to get herself into an upright position, she swiped at the mud on her gown and discovered it wasn't only wet and dirty, but torn in several places.

Even with considerable mending, she doubted it would be wearable again.

Ringing sounded in her ears. Had she hit her head?

Because the wind seemed to be carrying her name.

And that was impossible.

Rather than fall in the direction of the inn, she'd fallen away from it. Her limbs weren't broken, she was fairly certain, but they lacked the strength to get her moving again.

She went to draw in a breath, but instead choked and coughed.

Breathe, Addy, breathe. She'd leaned forward in an attempt to capture some wind in her lungs.

She'd vaguely remembered this happening when she was

younger, playing ball with some children in the village. The ball had slammed into her midsection and she'd fallen to the ground. The world had slowed down and she'd felt like she was underwater.

But she was not underwater now. She was on the side of a hill, somewhere between Warwick Crossing and London.

She glanced up to see Damien jumping and sidestepping toward her with a worried expression marring his beautiful face. Perhaps when she'd been rolling down the hill she'd hit her head after all.

Either that, or she was dreaming.

WOMEN!

$\mathscr{A}$s luck would have it, the taproom had failed to produce any games for Damien to distract himself. He'd been heading outside to the stables when one of the maids mentioned that Adelaide had said she might go walking

Alone.

Which meant it was his duty to bring her back.

Daft female.

He probably should not have commented on her friends' marriages while he was kissing her—especially when he'd been on the verge of doing more than kissing her.

He should have known better.

There weren't many places she could go, and Damien easily located a set of lady footprints leading away from the inn. Within ten minutes of walking, he spied her standing atop the nearby slope.

One second she was in his sights and the next she simply disappeared.

He realized immediately that the ground, which had

become waterlogged from all the rain, had simply washed out from beneath her.

His heart skipped a beat even before he'd taken off running and then it skipped another when, as he crested the rise, he saw her lying motionless at the bottom of the hill.

He'd only known her for a few weeks but seeing her there made his heart go cold.

"Adelaide!" he shouted. She didn't answer him, but at least she was moving now.

"Are you hurt?" Damien skidded to a halt. Dropping to his knees, he ran his hands along her arms and legs to ensure she hadn't broken anything.

She simply stared at him.

"Hurt?" she repeated. Ah, she'd had the breath knocked out of her.

"Breathe in, Addy. That's my girl." Her normally pale complexion was even more ghostlike but for the red scratches and dirt marring her delicate features.

Her strawberry blond hair, which had been secured in a neat chignon, was a riot of strands around her face.

"Another breath," he rubbed her back, willing the air she took in to fill her lungs.

"I'm all right," she managed, but Damien kept right on smoothing his palm over her shoulders and along her spine.

"Did you injure yourself anywhere else?" he grasped her wrists, gingerly turning them sideways and watching for her reaction. Nasty cuts, and a little swelling. But cuts had the potential to putrefy. "We need to get these cleaned up."

She gently pulled her hands away and met his gaze. "I'm sorry, Damien. It was all my fault—"

"You fell. It was an accident."

"No—before. Back at the inn. I don't know what came

ANNABELLE ANDERS

over me. I'm sorry for arguing with you. I know you didn't mean any insult by it. I just—"

Damien cut her off, claiming her mouth with his. She was all right. She was whole.

"No, I'm the one who is sorry," he murmured. For all of it. It had been his insistence on escorting her back to the townhouse that set all this in motion.

"I'm a selfish bastard," he added. Once he'd gotten over himself enough to realize his life wasn't the only one being upended, he'd considered the extent to which hers had been.

Adelaide enjoyed teaching and marrying him would bring that part of her life to an end.

But perhaps...

Perhaps it wouldn't be so bad after all.

He lowered her so she was lying in the grass beside him.

"Does it hurt anywhere?" he kissed the skin around her ears, and then down her neck. "Tell me where it hurts."

"No. No. Ah... But I'm sorry, Damien. Forgive me?"

He was kissing down her arm, and then back to her chin until he captured her mouth a second time. "There's nothing to forgive."

His cock strained against his trousers, and the last thing he wanted to do was stop where this was going, yet again. But...This was not the time for this.

She'd just taken a dangerous fall, by God. What kind of a cad was he?

If they were going to do this—if he was going to take this irrevocable step with her—he damn well wasn't going to do it on the side of a hill.

He gathered his self-control and pushed himself off her. Had he gone mad?

She blinked up at him as though she'd just realized where they were.

"What are you doing here? Did you come looking for me?"

Damien scrubbed his hand down his face. What were either of them doing here?

Rather than answering, he helped her back onto her feet. She wobbled some, but other than that, seemed capable of walking.

Or she would have been, anyway, if he'd been inclined to allow it.

Scooping one arm beneath her knees, he placed the other around her back, easily lifting her off the ground.

"I can walk!" Of course, she protested.

"Then why roll down the hill?" he asked deadpan.

"I just couldn't resist." Her eyes twinkled as she slid her arm around his neck.

"Ah, just as I thought. I'll have to keep better tabs on you next time."

Her good-natured humor impressed him.

And then she sighed.

"Oh, Damien," she sounded more than a little forlorn.

"Yes?"

"Just that. Oh, Damien."

She was silent for the remainder of the trek and when he lowered her onto the porch before entering, she simply smoothed her skirts and glanced over at him with those big green eyes of hers.

And thanked him.

With one more night to get through before they could be on the road again, she thanked him graciously.

Who was this young woman?

Hopefully, he'd know more of who she was by the time they conferred with her employer. As well as the repercussions of the Gazette's announcement.

One way or another, they'd be closer to some answers.

Trouble was, as he watched Adelaide climb the stairs, hips swaying, his muddy prints on the back of her skirt, Damien wasn't sure what he wanted those answers to be.

***

Addy expected Damien to follow her back to their chamber, but instead he sent her alone. And when she opened the door for a sharp knock shortly after, it wasn't for him, but the innkeeper's wife bearing soap and linens along with three servants carrying the same tub Damien had used the previous day.

A handful of trips and they'd trailed in and out with just enough buckets of hot water to fill it.

"Would you care for assistance?" One of the maids who normally worked in the kitchen hovered inside the door.

"No." Addy didn't want to keep the girl from her other chores. "Thank you."

Not knowing when Damien intended to return to their chamber, Addy had planned to keep her bath quick. But when he didn't return right away she found herself relaxing and soaking more than scrubbing and cleaning.

And eventually she simply leaned back, closed her eyes, and lost all track of time as the hot water went to work on her cuts and bruises.

"Adelaide? You aren't sleeping, are you?" His voice rolled through her like the sweetest of dreams. "Addy?"

She blinked her eyes open and slid them over to where Damien stood.

He'd carried her all the way back to the inn.

"I'm not sleeping." But she'd been close. So close, in fact, that it took her a minute to comprehend that Damien was standing only a few feet away from where she sat completely naked.

And when her gaze flicked around, she tried not to panic when she saw that she'd left the large linen towel draped on the bed, several feet away.

Damien noticed as well, and with a few steps snagged it up and crossed toward her.

"You didn't get much sleep last night either, did you?" He moved around to the back of the tub, quietly and with grace. *Her lion.*

Addy instinctively dunked lower in the water, holding a washcloth over her chest.

"Keep covered and I'll help get that soap out of your hair." He chuckled almost under his breath.

"You won't look?" She twisted around to meet his gaze.

"Not if you don't want me to." And, of course, he was sincere. He wouldn't lie to her. Already, she'd misjudged him earlier that day and look where that had gotten her.

Nodding, she closed her eyes, vaguely remembering her apology earlier. "I fell," she said.

"You did," he agreed as he poured warm water over her head. "Don't do that again, please? Don't go off on your own."

"You can't be with me all the time," she pointed out. At some point they were going to have to go their separate ways.

"Don't be so sure of that." He was scrubbing her back

now with a second cloth, squeezing water out and spreading it over her shoulders.

And as he stroked it over her skin, his touch transformed from comforting to something else—to something they'd both been dancing around all day.

WHERE DOES IT HURT?

*D*amien's groin tightened because he couldn't keep his gaze from following the tantalizing trail of bubbles sliding down her neck and onto her shoulders.

From the first time he'd been introduced to Miss Adelaide Royal he'd done his best to ignore this attraction. He'd done his best to deny this raw desire in him that cried out for this woman.

He'd almost fooled himself into believing he could succeed.

In fact, he'd gone so far as agree to escorting her back to Miss Primm's, convinced the attraction would fade upon acquaintance.

It had done the opposite.

Taken aback by his own thoughts, he tipped the last of the water and stepped back. The promise he'd made to Edgeworth had turned into something far more complicated than he'd imagined.

For most of his adult life, he'd avoided getting caught in

the matrimonial trap. He was not inexperienced when it came to resisting marriage minded women.

This, perhaps, was to be his greatest test of all.

With no soap to hide them, the scrapes she'd collected tumbling down the hill taunted him for his failure to protect her. His gut tightened and he couldn't help but reach out.

"Does it hurt?" he trailed his fingertip down one particularly long scratch.

"It'll fade. I'm glad you showed up when you did, although I could have walked back myself." She kept her eyes closed as she spoke and he noticed, not for the first time, the thickness and length of her lashes.

"Where does it hurt the most?"

A dusty rose color ebbed its way into her cheeks. "I'd rather not say."

Her derriere, then. "Poor Addy."

"Not Queen Adelaide?" This time she opened her eyes, sliding him a self-deprecating glance.

She leaned forward, hugging her knees, and exposed the gentle curve of her spine.

He dragged his fingertip beside another abrasion.

And although he wanted to follow the same line with his mouth, he held himself in check.

"You should dry off." The water was barely lukewarm.

"Close your eyes," she said.

The sun was still shining through the window and Damien was hopeful that the rain had moved on for good.

For now, anyhow, rain in England was never far off.

They'd spend one more night here. One more night.

"Close your eyes," she said.

The starchy little creature she'd been in London had

softened quite a lot. Somewhere along the literal and figurative road of their relationship, the lines had blurred.

He'd thought it would be simplest to check into the hotel as husband and wife. That had been a mistake. He should have claimed she was his sister, American accent be damned.

Stepping around to the side of the tub, he turned his head while holding the linen for her to step into. "I'm not looking. It's safe." But were either of them? He wasn't a monk, by God. His hands itched to explore the lush curves, slopes and contours he'd caught sight of.

Her movements were jerky as she swiftly covered herself. And he didn't step away until she'd assured him she was steady.

"I'll take dinner downstairs." He backed toward the door, adjusting his breeches which had become uncomfortably tight. "Don't wait up for me."

An accidental glimpse of tantalizing thigh almost stopped him from making his exit.

Almost.

The startled glance she sent from over her shoulder kept him moving.

A ROUGH NIGHT

*E*arly the next morning, Addy tamped down her frustration as she peered out the window of the coach. Damien and his mount, a considerable distance ahead of the coach, were barely in sight.

He'd not returned to their chamber the night before and her imagination had conjured up all sorts of possibilities for where he had spent the night.

In the stables where Coachman John lodged?

Had another chamber become available?

Or had he shared his bed with Becca? The maid who'd been ogling him over the course of their stay?

The coach hit a rut, reminding her of her bruises, and she wiggled on the bench seat trying to find a more comfortable position.

Perhaps he'd been kept warm by the older maid—the one who'd arrived outside their chamber early that morning with chocolate and biscuits.

A hint of humiliation irritated her. He had checked them into the inn as man and wife.

Fidelity wasn't a consideration for many married couples of the ton. It was one of the first things she'd learned upon coming to London.

And yet, she'd like to believe that despite their not actually being married, if Damien were to have a dalliance, he wouldn't make it a public one.

Regardless of where he'd slept the previous night, he'd kept his distance from her ever since her bath.

Was he still angry over their fight? But no, he'd kissed her on the hill.

Her suspicions made her queasy, which made no sense at all considering that they weren't really married.

They weren't anything, in fact.

Exhaling a loud sigh, she leaned back and turned her head to the window. Perhaps it was just as well.

No, not perhaps. It *was* just as well.

Because once they arrived at the school, all of this would be cleared up and he'd be on his way. Their paths would likely cross again, but not often. Only on special occasions that involved their mutual acquaintances.

He'd marry eventually, lords didn't have much choice.

What sort of woman would he wed? A sophisticated lady, one who knew how to oversee an estate—one with a decent sized dowry to be sure.

Not at all comfortable with this train of thought, Addy removed her book from the bag at her feet and escaped once again into a fictional world of Bartholomew Brown.

***

Outside, Damien shifted in his saddle.

He had not spent the previous night in the comfort of a

bed—alone or otherwise. And he had the aches and pains to support that.

After a rough few hours on the floor in the back of the taproom, Damien hoped to have squashed his urges where Adelaide Royal was concerned.

Those hours, however, had been spent in vain.

So not only did he sit atop his mount feeling somewhat sleep deprived, but in weaker moments, his thoughts drifted to inappropriate urges.

Making Damien stretch to loosen the fabric around his breeches.

Which was likely why Chaos stumbled on one of the muddier stretches.

"My fault, girl," Damien dismounted. "Easy, now." After running his hands along Chaos' haunches and legs, he surmised the injury wasn't serious.

Nonetheless, seeing as they were only a few miles from the school, he chose to lead the mare the remainder of the distance rather than add his weight to her burden.

He would not ride inside the carriage with Adelaide.

The exercise benefited not only his body, but also his mind, and by the time they arrived at the three-story building that housed Miss Primm's Private Seminary for the Education of Ladies, he had determined to face his circumstances head on.

Primm would demand they both acknowledge the truth. The circumstances brought about by the false announcement were nigh impossible to unravel.

And as Addy had pointed out, when it came to scandal, those who emerged unscathed normally only did so through one means of escape.

Marriage.

IT'S NOT FAIR!

*C*onflicting sentiments washed over Addy as they turned up the road that led to the school.

On one level she experienced the warmth of coming home and excitement to see familiar faces. But on another, more practical level, a cold terror seeped into her veins knowing she would learn her fate.

But perhaps she'd have a reprieve.

When Coachman John pulled them to a stop just outside Miss Primm's personal residence, a small group of ladies lingered outside the school itself.

Lady Rosewood, Miss Beatrice Wolcott, and of course Miss Primm. The others were not familiar.

Three looked to be somewhere in their thirties, slim and starched in grey gowns that could almost be uniforms. The fourth lady appeared closer to twenty. She was plump but the most animated and moved her hands wildly to emphasize her conversation.

But why were there four of them?

Before taking leave of the school nearly a fortnight

before with Chloe, Miss Primm had discussed the necessity of hiring replacements for three teachers: Victoria, now Lady Rosewood; Priscilla, now lady Hardwood; and Chloe who'd recently wed Captain Edgeworth.

Addy pushed away the tight sensation in her chest as she stuffed her book back into her bag. The fourth woman wasn't necessarily one of the new hires—likely she was the agent who'd scouted the teachers for Miss Primm.

That must be it. Addy evened her breaths, bracing herself while voices outside the carriage rose in greeting. Coachman John, Miss Primm, Miss Wolcott and... The door to the carriage flew open.

Damien.

For the first time all day he met and held her gaze showing more than casual interest.

"Are you ready for this?" he extended one hand, holding the door wide with the other.

"Are they teachers?" she shifted her glance to behind him, tamping down on her concern.

"Miss Primm has yet to provide introductions." But his mouth pinched together.

All Addy could do was nod and take his hand. "The fourth lady must be from an agency, or acting as companion." She spoke to reassure herself. "Or perhaps Primm's expanding the staff." It would make sense, having lost three teachers last term.

"Only one way to find out," Damien all but dragged her out of the coach.

Emerging into the setting sun, Addy twisted around and took note that a few construction workers hung off the side of the school, hammers in hand installing a new window.

"Not more vandalism, I hope?" She caught Beatrice's stare.

"Vandalism?" Beatrice flicked a meaningful glance toward their visitors. "There hasn't been any vandalism. We're just having the window replaced. Remember, it was damaged in the storm last month?"

"Oh, yes. Of course," Addy answered. An investigation had commenced just as Addy and Chloe left for London. Addy determined to pull Bea aside privately as soon as possible. As one of the only remaining teachers left from the original staff, she'd be able to catch Addy up on all the goings-on.

"Miss Royal," Primm was all business. "I've been wondering when you'd be so kind as to grace us with your presence again." The school director pinched her lips together, making her look older than her age, which Addy guessed to be around five and thirty.

Addy wished she could read Primm's expression better. Had the announcement in the Gazette reached Miss Primm's world?

"We experienced inclement weather—"

"And yet you are here now." Primm turned to the women she'd been walking with. "Would you be so kind as to excuse me for half an hour?"

"Of course, Miss Primm," the tallest of them dipped her chin.

"I'd be happy to show off our grounds," Beatrice shot Addy a sympathetic look before leading the visitors away. "The gardens are this way, ladies."

Damien touched Addy's arm and rather than duck her head in shame, she lifted her chin.

She would have expected herself to be overwhelmingly

intimidated under these circumstances. In fact, she'd all but imagined herself breaking into tears.

Why wasn't she? Damien gave her a reassuring squeeze.

Yesterday, he had emphatically insisted that the announcement wasn't her fault.

The reporter ought to have checked the church register to confirm his suspicions. Yes, Addy had thrown the flowers. But she'd not asked for any of this.

"This way, my lord," Primm gestured toward her residence, and then pinned her stare on Addy, "*my lady.*"

"Oh." But rather try explaining at this point, Addy followed her employer into her parlor.

Damien's good humor had returned from wherever he'd lost it for most of the day, and he politely accepted Primm's offer for tea.

Only after Primm's housekeeper stepped out of the parlor did Primm turn to Addy again.

Her sigh was weighty and loud.

"Did this relationship begin at Priscilla and Lord Hardwood's house party as well? I was certain Chloe was the only teacher I need worry about." She removed a folded newspaper from the table beside her—one that was all too familiar. "I don't suppose I'll allow my teachers to attend many house parties anytime soon."

"It's a mistake," Addy began. "The reporter saw us leaving the church after Chloe's wedding and wrote it up without authenticating their information."

"So there are no little viscountlings on the way?" Primm asked. "The two of you haven't fallen madly in love?"

"No ma'am," Addy was incapable of preventing the heat that rose to her cheeks. "No viscountlings of any kind."

"Miss Royal has acted with the utmost of propriety, Miss Primm," Damien asserted.

Primm's brows rose. "And where, pray tell, is Miss Royal's chaperone today? Has this mysterious woman chosen to ride in a second carriage that has yet to arrive? And before either of you answer, please keep in mind that my coachman is loyal to a fault."

"There is no chaperone. But we have been discreet," Damien answered. "Captain Edgeworth and I weighed the risks of a single young woman making the journey without protection. Coachman John is indeed capable, but he is only one man. We decided her physical safety trumped the risk of scandal."

Addy leaned forward. "It's not as though I'm a member of the *Ton*. My past has made my status in society irrelevant."

"But the school has a reputation to protect." Miss Primm studied Addy over her glasses. Ruthless, the woman's stare was positively ruthless. "I take it Lord Bloodstone has since obtained a special license?"

Addy began shaking her head. "No. No! The announcement was false. The viscount cannot marry me—"

"Is this true, Lord Bloodstone?"

"I'm more than willing to marry Miss Royal." He met Addy's gaze. "If necessary."

The room fell quiet at this point, with only the ticking of the clock to break the silence.

Miss Primm removed her glasses and rubbed the spot between her eyes before turning to Addy. "Addy, you know I cannot have a teacher who is involved in anything inappropriate, and being married but not married holds all sorts of potential for scandal."

"But—"

"The school is already in a tenuous position. Last year's issues… have left us more vulnerable than usual."

Addy had considered that Miss Primm might take this stance but not seriously.

The reality of being sacked hadn't occurred to her.

This was the one place where she'd experienced unconditional acceptance.

"But—" Panic fluttered in Addy's chest.

"I cannot risk it, Adelaide." Primm's hands remained folded in her lap.

This was happening. It was really happening. Primm was sacking her.

She was going to have to locate her father, or at the very least, follow her aunt to Bath.

Addy gripped the arm of the settee as though her life depended on it.

Was the earth falling out from beneath her or was that only her imagination?

"I'm sorry, Addy," Primm added. "Your students will miss you terribly."

But a replacement had already been found.

In the end, they were all replaceable.

Addy had been wrong to think she was prepared to face this. She wasn't at all ready.

She forced herself to stay calm.

"I suppose I have the rest of the summer to train my replacement…"

"Addy," Miss Primm tilted her head. "You cannot remain. I need you to cut all ties with the school until you've cleared up this situation."

"Cut all ties?"

"Lord and Lady Rosewood will put you and Lord Blood-stone up for the night. Following that, I ask that you leave the area. I am so very sorry, but I must put the school first."

A giant fist squeezed Addy's chest. This wasn't fair!

Miss Primm had gone out of her way to protect both Victoria and Priscilla last year! Although, Primm herself claimed at least some of the responsibility in both of those circumstances.

How was this any different?

Addy had gone to London to chaperone Chloe.

It wasn't fair!

"You needn't worry about Miss Royal," Damien inter-jected. "We'll travel together to Reddington Park where I'll make arrangements for a special license without delay."

Visible relief crossed Primm's expression. "Of course," Primm said, "Following an appropriate amount of time, both of you will always be welcome here." And then she added, "To visit."

But not to teach.

Married ladies did not teach at girls' boarding schools.

Addy bristled to be arranged by the two other people in the room. It was as though she wasn't even here.

Addy had already told him they couldn't marry. She'd already decided she would not allow Damien to compro-mise the stability of his estate by marrying her—a lady without a dowry.

She would travel with Damien to his home where perhaps she could act as a governess of sorts for his sister.

She could assist him with his reading issues. No, she was not without skills.

And while there, she would find a way to contact her father. She'd convince him to make a portion of her dowry available to her and then she'd make an independent life for herself.

She blinked away the stinging in her eyes. Never in all her life had she imagined Primm would sack her.

"Of course, I'll make my carriage and Coachman John available for the remainder of your journey."

"But what if we could convince the Gazette to run a retraction...?" Addy made one last feeble protest.

Primm was shaking her head.

"If you'll excuse me, ladies. I'll help Coachman John change out the horses." Damien rose and Addy sensed he was purposely allowing her and her employer—nay, former employer—a few minutes alone.

But what else was there to say?

"I'm so sorry, Addy. When I first saw the announcement, I questioned its validity. It just didn't sound like something you'd do. If I saw any other way out of this, I would have taken it, but I've already caused irreparable damage by sending Priscilla and Chloe to Hardwood Castle this past spring... I've no choice but to take the utmost of care." She shook her head. "For what it's worth, from what I've discovered, behind his very handsome visage, I'm to believe Lord Bloodstone is a decent man."

He was.

More than decent.

Which was precisely why Addy could not allow him to marry her.

AN IMPOSSIBLE SITUATION

*H*er limbs all but numb, Addy drifted from Primm's residence over to the school. Even after walking through the long hall and then climbing a long flight of stairs to the teacher's quarters, the stunned feeling remained.

"Is it true?" Beatrice met her at the door, wringing her hands. Seeing this particular colleague distraught brought the truth home.

Because a true calamity had to occur for Beatrice Wolcott to become ruffled.

"Where are the new teachers? They are replacement teachers, aren't they?" Addy asked.

"Yes." Beatrice winced. "They're returning to the inn to collect their belongings now, so you and I won't be interrupted. You must be exhausted. I'm so sorry, Addy. But although you are devastated, you must remember. The Bible doesn't say *this too shall stay*. It says *this too shall pass*. You will make it through this."

Despite having been walking outside, Beatrice's gown remained unwrinkled and her chignon tidy and neat. The calm and cool composition and literature instructor kept to herself more than any of the other teachers, but gave glimpses of a sensitive person inside. Addy had hoped that in time, they'd grow closer.

"Come sit down." She preceded Addy into the generously-sized teacher dormitory.

"Miss Primm didn't waste time in finding my replacement." Addy shook her head.

"She'd contacted the agency weeks ago. It was just lucky, I suppose, that they sent four qualified applicants for her to interview."

Not so lucky for Adelaide...

"When we saw the announcement in the Gazette," Beatrice continued, "rather than send the fourth lady away, Primm hired her to take over your classes."

Beatrice might just as well have stabbed a knife into Addy's heart.

"What happened?" Beatrice demanded, suddenly impatient with inconsequential details. "I read the announcement three times before I believed it."

"I had to read it five times," Addy said, biting her lip. She was uncertain as to who all she ought to share the truth with.

"You don't have to tell me." Bea stiffened beside her.

In the past, when any of the teachers had faced a difficulty of some sort, they'd turned to one another for help. Addy hadn't experienced anything that would keep her from sharing her secrets with them.

They had been like a small army, equipped with their

books and educations, intent on imparting knowledge that would allow their students to think independently.

And they'd been protective of one another.

With all that in mind, and needing to unburden herself to a sympathetic person, Addy outlined the general details of what had led her and Damien to their present unfortunate circumstances.

"You threw the flowers? As though you were the bride?"

"I didn't think of it that way. It was just that I had no need of them and I felt foolish carrying them. I didn't think..." Addy turned away to continue packing up her meager belongings.

"That horrid reporter ought to have verified such an important detail before printing an announcement. Have they no scruples whatsoever?" This was the most animated Addy had ever heard the other teacher.

"Lord Bloodstone asked them to print a retraction but they refused."

"Of course they refused. Doing so would only shed light on their own incompetence. I don't suppose it would matter, anyhow. Once the *Ton* sinks their teeth into a story like this, they aren't about to relinquish it easily. How outraged they must be to have another of Miss Primm's lowly teachers marry into the nobility!"

"But Beatrice, I can't marry him."

"Because your father cancelled your dowry?"

"Exactly. The viscount has financial responsibilities."

"But then what will you do?"

Addy had hoped Victoria would take her in, temporarily —until Addy could locate her father.

But then Primm requested Addy leave the area completely. *Out of sight, out of mind.* Addy understood the headmistress's reasoning. It was reminiscent of her aunt's philosophy. But that didn't make it sting any less. She was going to have to leave the one place she'd felt at home ever since her father brought her to England.

"His lordship has promised Primm we'd travel to his estate, and I'll not force him to break that promise—I'm going to speak with him about acting as governess to his sister until I contact my father. Papa will come through for me in the end. I'm certain. And there is always my aunt..." Addy was going to have to convince Damien once and for all that it was best they part ways.

Returning to London after having just travelled from there was a wearisome prospect in itself. Convincing Damien to accept her decision, quite another.

Beatrice turned to stare out the window. "I don't blame you for resisting the idea of marriage. One can never be certain a man's private character will match the one he shows the world."

But in Damien's case, Addy disagreed. "That's not my concern with Lord Bloodstone." In fact, she was more concerned that she'd be taking advantage of his good character to ensure her own security. In the short time she'd come to know him, she'd come to believe that he was one of those gentlemen who would cut off his right arm rather than act without honor.

"So you admire him?" Bea held her gaze.

"I do."

"Could you not convince your father to put up your dowry again?"

Addy shook her head. She had thought about this but in all the time she'd known her father, once he drew a line in the sand, he'd burn the world down rather than break his word.

Her dear papa wasn't one to ever admit he was wrong.

But Beatrice was going to have challenges of her own and Addy was tired of talking about herself. "What of you? Do you like the new teachers?"

Bea answered with a non-committal shrug. "I suppose. But it won't be the same."

"And the vandals? Have they been caught?"

"The Marquess of Sexton commenced an investigation and was here until a few days ago. I'd tell you more, but *his lordship* wasn't so amiable as to share his findings with someone so inconsequential as myself." Beatrice pinched her mouth together. "I believe he is following up on a lead."

The Marquess of Sexton was the oldest gentleman amongst Damien's colleagues and was one of the lords who'd travelled to the school. They'd all made a surprise visit when Captain Edgeworth had learned of Chloe's delicate situation.

"You don't seem impressed with him," Addy studied the other teacher. It wasn't like Beatrice Wolcott to express outward disdain for someone who was helping the school.

Or anyone, for that matter.

"That would be redundant because Lord Sexton esteems himself enough that no one else need ever do so." Beatrice smoothed the counterpane on one of the beds. "I do hope he nabs the culprit before the next session. It's unnerving knowing someone is out there who wants to harm the school."

"Are you afraid?" Addy asked. "For your own welfare?"

Just a few weeks before, someone had set fire to the students' dorms on the third floor. It had been sheer luck that Mr. Stewart, the architect working on Victoria and Lord Rosewood's estate, had been passing by at the time.

"I was initially, but since there've been no other incidents since then, I'm hopeful that whoever began this has decided it isn't worth the risk."

"Let's hope." Addy closed the trunk she'd packed up and glanced around. How was it that a lifetime's worth of belongings could fit into one medium-sized trunk?

She felt like she ought to be here to defend the school with Beatrice and the other teachers.

But she was no longer welcome.

Addy dragged her fingertips along the now empty wardrobe. She'd imagined this would be her home forever, but in the matter of a few weeks everything had changed.

She would spend a short amount of time at Damien's home, but then she'd move on—to London? To some village where no one had ever heard of her father?

Her father would help her. Wouldn't he?

The lack of control reminded her of being on the ship— subject to the wind, the sea, and the captain.

But this was not an adventure she'd planned for or wanted. Her home was no longer hers.

If worst came to worst, she could always return to America.

She blinked back tears. "I oughtn't keep Damien waiting."

"Damien?" Beatrice's brows shot up. "Are you sure there isn't something there that would be worth pursuing?"

Addy squirmed. She was not truly going to marry him.

Furthermore, regardless of any feelings between her and Damien, anything besides this unusual friendship they'd developed was out of the question.

"Lord Bloodstone," Addy corrected herself. "And no. He is perfectly charming, and perfectly honorable, so much so that sometime in the future, he will find some English lady who does not have a father withholding her dowry to marry."

A NIGHT AT LONGBOW

"*I*nterested in a wager?" Lord Rosewood handed a shining wooden cue across the felt table. The sun had long since set and the ladies had already excused themselves following dinner. This left Damien and the earl free to make use of the newly renovated Billiard room at Longbow Castle.

Damien vaguely wondered if Adelaide was going to go right to bed or stay up late confiding in Rosewood's countess. Would she tell her the truth?

Because Lady Rosewood had assigned he and Adelaide to a single chamber.

For all intents and purposes, he was married now.

"When will the restoration be finalized?" Damien watched as Piers Primm, the Earl of Rosewood, lined up a shot to initiate play.

The earl and his new countess had only recently purchased the crumbling castle from Lord Hardwood. They'd hired Rowan Stewart to head up the renovation, which was quite the coup. As a duke's bastard son, Stewart didn't require an occupation, but had made quite a name for himself nonetheless.

"By the time Stewart's completed everything, we'll need to start at the beginning again." Rosewood answered without removing the cigar from his mouth. The earl wasn't only heir to the Marquess of Starbridge, but he was also Miss Primm's younger brother.

Before marrying, Piers had been known as something of a rake.

"Handy fellow to have about," Damien commented. "Miss Royal tells me he's made most of the repairs at the school this past spring."

"*Miss Royal?*" Piers waggled his eyebrows mockingly as a puff of smoke wafted off the tip of his cheroot. "Best if you refer to her as 'my wife,' or 'my lovely viscountess'. Although I don't suppose it'll matter much once you got her safely tucked away up at Reddington Park."

Trouble was, Rosewood wasn't wrong.

The earl leaned over and lined up his cue. "If the truth gets out, ladies from all over Mayfair are going to start tossing wedding bouquets to capture a title." He slid the tip through his fingertips and sent two balls rolling into opposite corners.

"Trust me when I assure you that... *my wife*... had no ulterior motives if that's what you're implying. Nice shot, by the way." The words 'my' and 'wife' rolled off Damien's tongue easier than he'd imagined.

Rosewood cocked a brow. "If you say so."

"I do." Damien didn't want to argue with his host.

Bedding down at Longbow Castle for the night, even in light of the ongoing construction, was far superior to taking a chamber at any inn.

Damien couldn't help but recall the lumpy mattress he and Addy had shared two nights before, and the ineffective pillow used to attempt to affect a barrier.

The room had been dingy and one of the legs on the table had been shorter than all the others, and yet...

Where would matters be between them if the bed hadn't broken when it had?

If the luxurious furnishings on the main floor were any indication of how Lady Rosewood had outfitted the bedchambers, they'd not have any problem in that area tonight.

Damien studied the balls on the table and willed away ideas that had everything to do with that blasted bedchamber and nothing to do with billiards.

As it was, he and Adelaide hadn't resolved everything yet.

He had no doubt that Adelaide would have preferred to be sleeping in her small bed at the school, but she hadn't been given much choice.

Despite all the wishful thinking in the world, the most honorable Miss Primm had sacked her on the spot.

Two weeks ago, Damien would have expected Adelaide Royal to have collapsed in despair. But she was stronger than she looked—both physically and emotionally.

Neither her father nor her aunt had done anything to make her life easier.

Even Miss Primm had failed her.

Truth be told, Damien had expected more from the headmistress, considering Addy had been willing to put up her own money to shore up the school.

Which reminded him... "Has Sexton found any leads to

track down whoever's been terrorizing your sister's school?"

In lieu of a few similar acts of vandalism at other institutions, the Marquess of Sexton had taken it upon himself to look into the matter.

"He's following one now." Rosewood frowned. He didn't seem all that happy about whatever the marquess had discovered.

"What is it?"

Rosewood stared down at the felt table. "A stranger was seen loitering around the inn in Warstone Village the week surrounding the fire—for no apparent reason."

"Did someone get his name?"

"Not his name, but a good description." Rosewood clamped his mouth together, almost as though he'd rather not divulge his suspicions.

"This stranger stayed at the inn for three nights, and when he departed he failed to take all his belongings with him."

They'd presumed the arsonist hadn't been all that intelligent when he'd left an abundance of evidence at the fire. But this... this could actually lead to something.

"And what was concluded from them?" Damien asked.

Addy would be tremendously relieved if the culprit was found and stopped. She may no longer be employed by Miss Primm but that didn't mean she'd stopped caring for the school.

"An envelope. The seal was broken but intact. But it's the stamp that troubles me: stars in a circle that overlaps a lion."

"But that's your—"

"My family crest. The envelope came from Starbridge Abbey."

171

"It could be a mistake." If it came from Starbridge Abbey, that meant that Miss Primm's own family had set out to sabotage her school.

"It could be a mistake," Damien pointed out.

"It could be. But what if it isn't?"

ANOTHER BACKUP PLAN

"Come in," Addy turned away from the window to greet whoever was at the door. The guest chamber was one of the newly completed ones at Longbow Castle and the décor was a far cry from the chamber she and Damien had shared the night before.

Damien stepped in, and after closing the door silently behind him, he held her gaze and cocked a brow. Warmth spread through her limbs and for the first time all day, Addy didn't feel as though her world had fallen apart.

"She was adamant then?" he asked. Meaning their hostess's insistence that the two of them share a single chamber.

"She was."

With a shrug, Damien tossed his jacket over a chair and then reached to loosen his cravat.

"Most of their servants are new," Addy explained. "Victoria couldn't guarantee their discretion."

After Addy had poured out her story again for the umpteenth time that day, Victoria had pointed out that since they'd already shared a room once, suspicions were more likely to take root if a hastily married couple chose *not* to share a chamber.

"And you're going to marry him anyway." Victoria had said.

"She's not wrong." Damien flicked a glance toward the bed and Addy fought off the part of her wishing this was real.

"We can't marry, Damien." She had prepared herself for this argument.

"If that's what you want. We'll have to come up with an alternative plan once we've arrived at Reddington Park then."

Addy's jaw nearly dropped at his easy acquiescence. At the very least, she'd expected a token resistance.

His reaction shouldn't be as disappointing as it was.

"I'll introduce you to my mother and my sister. I had considered sending Caledonia to Miss Primm's but I'm not comfortable until the vandal has been caught. You'd be providing a tremendous help if you'd be willing to step in as her governess."

"You would hire me as your sister's governess?"

"For the time being. Why not?"

Not that she wanted to talk him out of his offer but... Well, at this point, "I'm hardly a stellar example of a lady."

Damien waved a hand through the air. "Throwing wedding flowers is hardly cause to be shunned," he said.

"But not everything we've done was innocent." It was the first time that day either of them had mentioned the improprieties they'd shared at the inn.

"Do you regret it?" he asked, pausing to unbutton his waistcoat. How was it that she felt perfectly normal watching him disrobe like this?

If she acted as his sister's governess, that would make him her *employer*.

But he'd asked her a question and was waiting for her answer.

"Did you?" she shot back at him.

"No."

She wasn't sure what she'd expected but such a stark answer wasn't it. A *perhaps*, or maybe a similar hedge to hers.

"But," he continued, "As long as we keep this between you and me, it doesn't really matter, does it?"

"It doesn't?"

"Not if you don't want to marry me." He lowered himself onto a plush velvet chair and began removing his boots. Should she step forward to help him? That wasn't something any governess would ever do.

"It isn't that I don't *want* to marry you." She emphasized the word want. There was so much more to it than that.

"So you *do* want to marry me."

"No," she answered.

"If you don't want to marry me, then why are you staring at me like that?" Did the corner of his mouth twitch? She couldn't tell because he was sitting and looking down, removing his boots.

"Like what?"

"Like I'm a cherry-covered truffle." The corner of his mouth was definitely twitching now.

"I am not," she insisted. "And it is *you* who doesn't wish to be married to me."

"I never said that." His violet eyes flashed up at her. "I've expressed my desire to marry you more than once, now."

"No, you said you were *willing* to marry me. Willing and wanting are two distinctly different emotions."

She stared down at the stockinged foot where he'd successfully removed one of his boots.

"If I'm willing to be married to you, why aren't you willing to be married to me?"

Addy blinked, and then she frowned. "Don't you have a valet?" She'd thought all titled gentlemen employed valets.

"I sent Mr. Burke home the night before we left London. He'll be waiting at Reddington Park when we arrive. Can't wait to introduce you." Another twitch.

"Why would you send him away?"

"I didn't need him." And then he made that slow smile that never failed to weaken her knees. "I had my wife with me."

And in the midst of what she had considered an argument, on a day when she'd been sacked and kicked out of her home at the same time, she inexplicably found herself grinning at him.

"There's that smile," he said. "You've had a difficult day."

But something loosened inside her.

Despite the troubles he would surely have to face over all of this, he'd been conscious of her feelings.

She would miss that about him.

And as though to emphasize the strength of the feelings she was developing for this man, her heart skipped a beat when he crossed the room. And it skipped another when he gathered her into his arms. "I'm sorry you lost your position."

As a viscount, Damien lived in an altogether different world. He moved in circles where she would never fit.

Why, then, was he the person who had shown her the most compassion?

Addy buried her face in his shoulder, memorizing his scent as she did so. Something spicy, soap, bergamot, and a hint of cigar smoke.

As his sister's governess, there would be no more hugs, no more kisses, and no more special looks shared between the two of them.

Damien tilted her head back so she had no choice but to look into his eyes. Like a flint to stone, the air between them charged.

He searched her expression with his violet gaze. What did he see?

This time their mouths met in an urgent, almost violent kiss and that wall he'd kept between them all day instantly crumbled.

It shouldn't. He shouldn't.

She shouldn't.

Their teeth clashed and the whiskers of his beard scraped her skin.

And she couldn't get enough of it.

Damien released her mouth to trail around her jaw and chin almost frantically. "This wasn't supposed to happen, Addy. This isn't in my plan. *You* aren't in my plan."

"I know." She threaded her fingers through his hair. Tears burned behind her eyes, not because she was sad or disappointed, just overwhelmed.

She could lie with him tonight, take that final step, and again, no one would know what transpired between the two of them.

But he was confusing her.

He'd treated her with tender affection after she'd fallen

177

down the hill and then he'd shifted into a very different sort of person—he'd treated her with a cool distance afterward. And she'd worried when he'd not returned to their chamber the night before.

She leaned away to see his expression, her fingers unconsciously thrumming his chest.

"Why were you angry with me last night? And today?" It cannot have been the fight she'd picked with him before storming out for her walk. He'd said he forgave her for that.

He'd become angry after he'd rinsed her hair.

"I wasn't angry with you."

"But you were angry."

"Yes." His throat moved. "With myself."

"Because I'm not in your plans."

"Yes." He exhaled, but then pulled her against him. "But I've realized something."

With his hard form warming her from chest to thighs, she had to concentrate to hear his words over the rush of blood roaring in her ears.

"What have you realized?" she asked when he didn't answer right away.

He smoothed his hand down her back. She startled when he splayed his palm over the flesh just below her waist. "We're inevitable."

"We are?"

"This." He ignored her question, walking her backward until her thighs bumped the tall bed. "Is inevitable."

"It is?"

He captured her mouth again, thoroughly exploring hers. "Um hm…" He was done talking.

"Oh," Addy tilted her head back so he could trail his mouth down her neck and to the top edge of her night rail.

She did not stop him when he unfastened the buttons, or when he palmed his hand over her breast.

She did not stop him when he moved his mouth from one nipple to the other, or when he sucked at the tip, tugging, and then scraping his teeth over the sensitive skin.

Her desire to open herself up to this man encompassed her completely.

Had this been fated all along?

He lifted her onto the mattress, crawling half over, half beside her.

And even as his mouth worshiped every inch of skin he could get to, his hands smoothed over her curves. Being touched by this man felt so very good.

Everything he did felt so very good.

Better than her favorite book—better than a secret swim at the height of summer.

Better than *chocolate*.

Damien's hand hovered low on her belly, just above where she'd clenched her thighs together. "Open for me."

So much heat there. Liquid hot desire.

"What are you going to do?" Was this something they should discuss together first?

"Trust me."

She relaxed her muscles and his fingertips dipped lower, gathering the fabric of her night rail, exposing her most intimate place.

"Consider this my apology." His breath sent a shiver through her. Not because it was cold. She was as far from cold as a person could possibly be.

"Apology?"

"For being an ass."

He covered her mound and his fingers slicked through her folds.

Perhaps today wasn't so bad after all.

***

Several months had passed since Damien had been with a woman. Not because he'd consciously denied himself, but because he'd simply been distracted.

There had been times in his life when that would have bothered him more, but he'd focused most of his time and attention on the brewery and his estate.

But tonight, he was one hundred percent focused on Adelaide.

He teased her opening, eliciting a quiver. Knees that had been locked together a minute before opened wide for him.

Damien couldn't remember the last time he'd been this excited, this hungry to devour a woman.

Was it because he was going to have to marry her? He would have thought he'd experience the opposite.

It's because she is Adelaide.

Sliding between her folds, he explored velvety flesh. Wet, warm, welcoming.

And when she breathed a sigh of appreciation, he greedily captured her soft exhale in his mouth. "You're so beautiful." He stroked her inner walls.

"No." She arched generous hips off the bed, moving with him now, and he added a second finger. He pushed deeper even as he imagined that it was his cock stretching her—filling her.

Fucking her.

He'd had similar thoughts on several occasions now—

when she'd slept beside him. When they'd been in the carriage alone together.

When she'd been sitting in the tub—injured and tired. What the hell was wrong with him?

She trusted him.

One of his best friends had asked him to protect her and he'd failed spectacularly.

Resting his head on his elbow, working his hand at her center, Damien studied his little American.

Strands of strawberry blonde hair had been braided but the shorter lengths caressed her forehead, her cheeks and jaw.

She reminded him of a butterfly. Close up, her pale skin almost translucent. And her lips were as soft as rose petals.

She stilled, opened her eyes, and slid him a wary glance. "You're watching me."

She stared at him as though he'd not only hung the moon but plastered the sky with the stars.

He didn't deserve such adoration.

This was the least he could do.

"I like watching you," he said.

She shook her head and her brows came together as though she didn't believe him.

Damien could not have that.

"Do you know…" He curled his fingers inside. "What touching you…" He slid them over her most intimate flesh. "Does to me?"

She shook her head, her gaze locked with his.

He thrust his cock against her hip and her pupils expanded.

"It excites me. Damn, Adelaide, *you* excite me." He plunged both fingers deeper, curling them. She appealed to him more than a practiced courtesan. She was more alluring than the most sought-after debutante.

He'd tried denying this attraction from the moment he'd been introduced and failed quite spectacularly.

Her lashes swept down, hiding emerald depths, and her lips parted on a faltering gasp.

Providing bliss for this woman, he realized, pleased him immensely.

"What—" She licked her lips. "Why me? What about me excites you?" she asked.

Where to begin.

"Your mouth excites me," he claimed it, mimicking the movements of his hands, stroking the inner walls with his tongue.

Addy twisted and bowed, her hands gripping his shoulders.

He moved his mouth lower, capturing and then laving one rosy tip into a tight bud, pinching the other with his free hand.

"Your breasts excite me." He would lose himself in them if he could.

She was close to finding her release and he relished her growing tension.

Even as he sucked her into his mouth, he dragged his thumb over her clit.

Feminine muscles clenched, and he pushed deeper. She cried out, exposing the perfect line of her neck, her mouth twisted in an expression of half-pleasure, half-pain.

"Beautiful," he whispered in awe, giving her what she needed to find complete satisfaction.

And loving every second of it.

His little American—his sweet Adelaide

TO BE A WIFE OR A GOVERNESS

*T*ime lost all meaning and Addy lie limp as a rag doll. She barely moved, in fact, even when he removed his hand from between her legs.

Only after he'd snuffed out the candles and returned to bed did she turn to snuggle beside him.

"That was a rather impressive apology," she spoke into the darkness, remembering what he'd said when he began.

But that wasn't all it was, was it?

Chloe had confided to Addy that she'd entered an affair with Captain Edgeworth purely for the sex. And yes, she had called it *sex*. So Addy was aware that there were physical aspects of it that had nothing to do with procreation.

Or emotion.

According to Chloe, entering into the affair had been as simple as admitting their mutual attraction and deciding to act upon it.

This, whatever it was, however, that was unfolding between herself and Damien, was far from simple.

For the first time in almost a decade, she truly mourned

the losses she'd incurred when her father cancelled her dowry.

Was Damien to be yet another loss? But how could he be a loss when he was only here because he had to be?

He'd told Primm he would marry her, but had then accepted her refusal graciously.

Too graciously?

"Shh…" Damien touched her lips. "You're thinking very loudly."

Without consciously doing so, she touched her tongue to the tip of his finger.

She ought to be repelled by the taste.

Salty. Unique.

Her.

When had she become such a wanton?

She sucked, sliding it inside, and he groaned.

"God, Addy." He removed his hand and rolled over so that he was on his side, still embracing her. "Don't you want to sleep?" he asked.

But in this position, she was acutely aware of his arousal. She had even more questions now than she'd had five minutes ago.

There was no way she was going to be able to sleep.

"Ha," she said. But the darkness in the room provided her cover to be blunt. "What do we do now?"

"You said you didn't want to marry me."

"I know, but…" Her eyes were wide open, staring into nothing. "We can't do this if I'm going to be your sister's governess."

"Then be my wife."

"But we've been over this," Addy pointed out. "What about your back-up plan? You know I don't have a dowry."

"I'll come up with a different back-up plan." But he sounded sleepy. They'd both had a long day of travel and he'd made that promise to Primm.

It was obvious that he wasn't thinking this through.

"Why didn't you…" Addy swallowed, not wanting to sound like the clueless spinster that she'd always considered herself to be. "Why didn't you put yourself inside?"

She had been willing. Even now, she marveled at how her surrender had been so complete.

"You still have choices this way," he settled into his pillow. "Addy?"

"Hmm?" His chest rumbled beneath her cheek.

"We have another long day tomorrow. Sleep first. We'll figure everything out later."

But what were those choices? And what other back-up plans could he possibly come up with?

Unfortunately, and most annoyingly, his breathing turned even.

He was asleep.

All those questions would have to wait until tomorrow, when, presumably, they would take to the road once again.

And when they arrived at their destination she'd meet his mother and his sister. Addy had seen Reddington Park from a distance, of course, when she'd attended Priscilla's wedding at Hardwood Cliffhouse. But she'd never been invited inside.

And Addy found some solace that she'd have Priscilla for a neighbor.

But the biggest question of all remained to be answered. Would she arrive as Damien's wife, or as a new governess for his sister?

***

The next morning dawned clear and bright.

"I look forward to reading your letters," Victoria gave Addy a tight hug as they made their goodbyes beside the waiting carriage.

True to her promise, Primm had made her personal carriage along with Coachman John available to Addy and Damien once again. Addy had travelled the day and a half-long trip earlier that summer for Priscilla's wedding at Hardwood Cliffhouse and hoped the newly married couple would have returned from their honeymoon.

The thought temporarily lifted her spirits.

Her spirits lifted higher, however, when Damien climbed into the carriage beside her.

"You aren't going to ride today?"

He adjusted his jacket so he could sit more comfortably, and then frowned. "Chaos strained a ligament in the mud yesterday. I'm going to leave her in Rosewood's stable until she heals."

"Oh, no! I didn't realize!"

He patted her hand. "She'll be fine. She reared back and slipped. My fault, of course. I should have known she'd get frustrated with the road conditions."

"Did you know she'd injured it?"

"I suspected. But I wasn't sure until I saw that the joint was inflamed this morning."

"Is it serious?" His horse was more than a means of transportation for him.

"I don't think so, but Rosewood assured me he'd send for his veterinarian to examine her." Damien did not look pleased.

"You don't like leaving her. We can wait, can we not?" But she caught herself a second after the suggestion flew out of her mouth.

Because they could not.

And that was because of her—because Miss Primm had asked her to leave the area.

He made another grim smile.

"She'll be fine. I trust Rosewood to provide excellent care. His stables are proof of that."

"I'm sorry, Damien."

"Adelaide," he pinned his gaze on her. "You did not make it rain in England for two days. You did not force Chaos to act out. You did not make it imperative that we leave today. Do you know what I'm saying?"

She bit her lip. "That Chaos' injury is not my fault?"

"Exactly." The carriage jerked and then moved forward and Damien slid his arm along the back of the bench.

"Well, I'm sorry she is injured," she added. "Regardless."

He chuckled under his breath and Addy contemplated whether or not she had the courage to lean into him.

They had been intimate the night before—*very intimate.* Had that been a one-time thing? And if not, was affection to be limited to the bedchamber?

She pondered how one went about approaching such questions while staring at the horizon. They might get sprinkled on but the clouds ahead weren't nearly as ominous-looking as the ones they'd been caught in two days before.

She hesitated in asking her questions outright because when she woke up in that huge bed, she'd been alone.

He'd gone out. Had he been anxious to get away from her?

She'd learned he'd spent the morning in the stables with Lord Rosewood while breaking her fast with Victoria.

Because his horse had been injured.

The brief separation however, in light of… everything… had set her on edge.

"You'll visit soon. Once all this is in the past. I promise."

How did he always seem to know what she was thinking?

Addy sent him a questioning look.

"Unless you don't want to," he added. "Are you angry with Miss Primm for sacking you?"

Addy rolled her lips together. Was she angry with Primm?

"No," she admitted. "I understand. I do. I guess I just thought I'd work at the school forever."

She wasn't angry but she did feel hurt.

"No back-up plan?" He lowered his arm around her shoulders.

Addy shook her head and allowed herself to relax a small amount.

"No back-up plan." But when Coachman John turned onto the road that led away from town, she sighed.

"But the experience is quite unpleasant—being fired." Being sent away from a place she'd considered home for nearly a decade brought up unwanted feelings from the past.

She'd not confided her feelings to Victoria, having worn a brave face for the length of their short visit. She hadn't wanted any more of the other woman's pity. She didn't want anyone's pity.

Damien's hand stroked her arm.

"She didn't have a choice, you know." His voice sounded almost too soft for her to hear.

Gentle.

Adelaide knew this. And she'd thought she was immune to self-pity, but knowing all of that failed to dull the cut of rejection.

How many times had important people in her life rejected her? Losing her mother wasn't technically a rejection, but it had felt like one.

It still felt like one.

And then her father had abandoned her to her aunt, who, following Marcus' rejection, had demanded Addy find somewhere else to live. Not to mention that most of the *Ton,* people she'd considered to be her friends, had refused to meet her stare.

She'd put all of that behind her.

She had not prepared herself for this rejection, however, not from Miss Primm.

"It's difficult not to take it to heart."

She hated that it bothered her so much.

"She didn't fire you because you weren't good enough." Damien turned so she had no choice but to meet his stare. "Her reasons had very little to do with you. She needs to protect the school."

"I do know this, *I do.*" She pinched her mouth together. He did not understand! How could he? He was not only a man, in a world built around men, but he was a viscount.

"I can't imagine you know what rejection feels like."

He frowned. He was trying to be nice to her and she was being contrary. But she'd not take her words back. Because deep in her heart she couldn't imagine him ever being as familiar with rejection as she was.

"Then you would be wrong." His words were short.

How could she be wrong? It wasn't that he didn't understand, but he couldn't understand.

He had been born with everything. He was Lord Damien Reddington, for heaven's sake. "Who would ever reject you?" Addy asked, not stopping to wonder if such a question might be too personal. "Just look at you."

She blushed at her words. Why did she do this? Why did she pick fights with him?

But just as she went to apologize, he broke the silence first.

"You're too quick to judge, Adelaide. I wouldn't have expected that of you."

She hated that he sounded disappointed. "What other assumption would you have me make? You are a viscount!"

He exhaled a harsh laugh.

"Is that all you think I am?" He turned away from her, crossing his foot over his knee. Was he pretending he didn't care?

"Of course not." Was she so shallow as to never look beyond the outside trappings of his identity? And yet...

What pain could he possibly be hiding from the rest of the world?

Is that all you think I am?

His question shamed her.

"I'm sorry. I shouldn't assume."

They rode with neither of them talking again for a good two or three minutes before he broke the silence.

"My father betrothed me to the daughter of his oldest and dearest friend," he said.

"But you are not married," she pointed out the obvious and he exhaled another short laugh.

"Aren't I?" He caught her glance with raised brows before turning to face front again.

"Well, not really," Addy bit her lip, waiting for more of his explanation. He seemed to require a moment to collect his thoughts.

"Christine was two years younger than me. I wasn't yet twenty. St. George's was packed—as were the surrounding streets. It was to be the wedding of the Season and my parents couldn't have been more pleased. But it was not meant to be..."

Addy hadn't realized she was holding his wrist. She squeezed it. It was something he'd done more than once to comfort her.

"That morning, my father told me he'd never been more proud." Damien's mouth tightened. "Joining our families was something he'd wanted all his life."

"Oh, Damien."

"She left me standing at the altar."

"She *what?*"

"She sent me a note—a flowery explanation of why she could not marry me. Unfortunately, I didn't take the time to read it."

Flowery.

Addy pictured handwriting with loops and swirls, and a nervous young man on his way to a church filled with upstanding members of the ton.

"What were her reasons?"

"She was in love with her tutor. They eloped, as I understand it, and now live in the country quite happily on a stipend provided by her father."

"She married her tutor? Rather than you?"

"He was a great lover of literature. Something the two of them had in common." He stared out the window.

"So you do know rejection," Addy sighed. "I'm sorry."

"It was a long time ago." He shrugged.

Addy studied his back. Despite his bravado, he could not have enjoyed dwelling on it again.

"Thank you for telling me."

And again, he shrugged. "It's in the past."

He was embarrassed.

And he was proud.

But Addy read between the lines. He'd not read Christine's note because, overcome with nerves as he'd been that morning, he could not take the time to decipher her handwriting.

Christine.

The woman had been a fool to reject such a man as Damien Reddington.

"Did you love her?"

He was handsome and charming and all the things she'd imagined him to be, but he was also...Damien.

In the few short weeks since they'd been introduced, his golden hair had grown longer, lending him a devil-may-care look as a few locks curled around his chiseled jaw.

The twin shadows etched below his violet eyes accentuated a tiredness she hadn't noticed before.

And in unguarded moments, he clenched his jaw.

She had brought about these changes—she had upended all his plans.

Just when she thought he wasn't going to answer, he finally spoke.

"I was in awe of her. I admired her. She was a fragile and beautiful girl whom I'd taken for granted all my life, but I didn't love her." He ran a hand through his hair. "The worst of it was disappointing my father."

And then he removed his arm from around her, stretching, stiffening in a manner that signified he was finished with this discussion.

She'd hated when people made assumptions about her because she was American, and now she'd done the same to him.

There was a good deal about this man that she didn't know. Would she ever have the chance to really know him?

"YOU'D KNOW IF I KISSED YOU."

*D*amien could have borrowed one of Rosewood's mounts, or even ridden on the driver's box with Coachman John.

But Addy was the sort of woman who, when left alone, succumbed far too easily to the weight of her thoughts.

And left to ride alone in the carriage, no doubt she'd borrow trouble beyond their realm.

He hadn't realized, however, that riding with her would result in him blathering over something that happened years before.

The weeks following the wedding that never was had been the only time in his life when he'd truly borne his father's disappointment. His father had refused even to listen to Damien's apology.

"Why would your father be disappointed in you if she was the one who broke it off?" Addy asked, apparently not finished with this conversation.

Damien wasn't going to spell out to her that his fiancé

had wanted to spend her life with someone more intelligent.

"My father insisted that I should have been able to do something." He shook his head. He could have courted her more ardently. He could have written poetry for her.

Complimented her more.

"You can't take the blame for her decision," Addy declared and then pinched her mouth together. "Not unless you wish me to take the blame for Miss Primm's."

Damien clamped his mouth closed.

Even though she wasn't completely right, she had a point. It was never pleasant when the person you were arguing with used your own reasoning against you.

"Very well," he leaned back and then eyed her bag. "Did you bring your book?"

Apparently as willing to move to another subject as he was, she reached down to her bag. "I did." She brightened considerably.

And as they rode the next several miles along that endless highway, she read aloud, occasionally pausing to discuss some particular event or question in the story.

And Damien listened.

And watched her.

And simply wondered that somehow, despite everything, this woman was coming to mean a good deal to him.

Which only managed to push his back-up plan back a little further.

***

Addy relaxed onto the blanket she'd spread out over the grass and stared at the sky.

"I'll be happy not to ride in a carriage for the rest of the year," she declared.

She and Damien had stopped to enjoy the basket of food Victoria had sent along while Coachman John watered the horses.

She would not have expected to enjoy the first part of this journey, and yet sharing her book with Damien more than doubled the enjoyment she normally got from reading.

As a person who often preferred solitude, this struck her as intriguing.

Was this what marriage was like?

Victoria was happy with Lord Rosewood—more than happy, in fact. Was it possible one could enjoy all the normal entertainments even more if they could share them with the right person?

She turned and stared at where Damien lie on the ground beside her. He appeared particularly relaxed, his eyes closed and his mouth parted softly.

He'd shared his rejection with her and they'd managed to move beyond it.

She'd allowed unmentionable liberties the night they spent at Victoria's house, but this…

Felt like friendship.

Aristocratic marriages weren't arranged with compatibility as a factor. What would it be like if people simply married who they wanted?

She closed her eyes and had nearly drifted off to sleep when something brushed her lips. She swiped a hand at it, and not finding anything, opened her eyes.

Damien hovered over her. "We need to pack up," he said.

"Did you just kiss me?" she asked, not moving.

He waved the stem of a daisy he was holding and sent her a slow grin. "You'd know if I kissed you."

"Would I?" Her breath caught.

Such a taunt was perhaps the most daring thing she'd ever said. She knew she'd provoked him when his eyes darkened.

But Coachman John awaited them. The road was only a few hundred feet away. The sound of a horse neighing provided a distant warning.

Addy gathered the utensils and leftover food while Damien folded the blanket. But rather than gesture for Addy to precede him toward the carriage, Damien took the basket from her and then, bending forward, threw her over his shoulder.

"Damien!" She couldn't help laughing as she feigned a token protest. "What are you doing?"

"Simply gathering up my belongings."

"*Belongings?*" His using the word in context with her, although she ought to feel insulted, sent a carnal thrill racing down her spine.

"That's right." Humor rumbled in his voice as he marched across the meadow.

"And who do you belong to?" she asked.

"Who do you think?" She wasn't sure if the buzzing in her head came from his answer or the fact that she was hanging upside down.

Because the buzzing swooshed away when he lowered her feet to the ground.

"Are you well, Miss Royal?" Coachman John's question sent heat flooding back into her cheeks.

"I am well, thank you, Coachman," Addy shot Damien as

much of a reproachful glance as she could summon while climbing back into the carriage.

And recalling all the rules they'd broken this past week, she couldn't help but blush.

They had not been acting properly and no matter how many people had read that blasted article, she and Damien were not married in truth.

Having tied the basket onto the back, Damien climbed in beside her. But this time, he took the back-facing seat, sitting across from her as the coach drew back onto the road.

"Your father will think you've married." His comment was one Addy hadn't allowed herself to dwell on.

"Yes." Addy kept her stare focused on his.

"And your aunt."

She nodded. "As well as your mother and sister and all of your friends."

"I don't think you really want to be employed as my sister's governess, do you?" One corner of his mouth lifted.

"Don't I?"

"What do you want, Addy?"

You. The thought jumped into her head before she could stop it. Thankfully, she'd managed to keep it from flying out of her mouth.

"I don't know," she said instead.

She wanted to know the future. She wanted to know what her father thought about all of this, but most of all… Addy inhaled a fortifying breath.

"I want you to kiss me again."

Before she could take in a breath, Damien was across the carriage obliging her request.

BACKUP PLAN BE DAMNED

*D*amien released her mouth and waited for her to meet his gaze.

"What do you want, Adelaide?" he asked again.

She blinked. "Why do you call me Adelaide? You can call me Addy if you'd like." She avoided his question.

"I will. Occasionally. But most of the time I want to savor it—hold your name in my mouth longer. Hell, I want to savor everything about you." And then he repeated. "What do you want, Adelaide?"

She'd had her arms around his neck, but moved one hand to the side of his face.

"I don't know." Damien barely heard her whisper over the crunching of the carriage wheels.

Damien had noticed the desire in her eyes when she'd stared up at him in the meadow.

Her pupils had dilated and her cheeks flushed. If he hadn't caught sight of Coachman John out of the corner of his eyes, he'd have kissed her thoroughly right there.

Kissing the woman was a revelation. In his arms, she blossomed like a flower in the sunlight.

And the two of them were alone, in the carriage, with nothing but time on their hands.

"Do you want me to savor you?"

He wouldn't push her. Already she'd been backed into more than she could ever have foreseen.

"You want to savor me?"

He could make excellent use of their time.

"What does that mean?"

"Should I show you?"

"I think so." Another whisper. "Yes. Will you?"

It was all the enticement he required. His hand was already sliding her skirts out of the way as he kissed a trail from the corner of her lips to the hollow between her breasts.

"Here first." He moved his mouth to her right breast, nipping, licking, and then sucking at the turgid bud and was surprised to feel his heart racing.

"Please," she gasped. "Yes." He loved the sound of her voice, especially when it was all breathy and needy.

He stopped to take in his handiwork where the nipple glistened from his mouth. He hardened at the thought of other rosy glistening places he would claim.

Shifting his stare to her face, he watched her expression transform as he glided his hand across her thigh.

"I want to savor you here." He drew lazy circles on tender skin. She widened her legs for him.

"And here." He stroked the petals at her opening.

She was his for the taking. But rather than move directly to the main course, he tugged at her gown, exposing her other breast in order to grant it equal attention.

"*Damien.*" He loved his name on her lips. "We shouldn't, should we? What if... Ahh...But," she seemed to be arguing with herself. "Everyone thinks we're married anyway."

He chuckled at her one-sided conversation.

"True." He teased her opening and thrust one finger inside. Satisfaction surged to his chest when a flush ebbed up her neck.

She gasped and clenched around him.

"Not yet, my Adelaide." His cock hard as steel, he shifted her off his lap and dropped to his knees before her.

He wouldn't take her in a coach. No, he'd have her in his bed.

Because he *would* have her. She'd be his wife in truth. He'd grown more certain of that each day.

Back-up plan be damned.

For now, he'd worship her with his mouth.

But as he knelt between her legs, she stared down at him with a mixture of embarrassment and anticipation.

And lust. He'd not discount the naked lust in her eyes.

"I wish you could see yourself." He pushed her gown up and out of the way. "Open and so damn willing, baring yourself for me."

Her throat moved as she deliberated his words.

"You're wicked," she finally whispered.

"So are you." He edged his hands higher on her thighs, pushing her legs wider as he did so. "Do you know how beautiful you are?" His gaze moved from her breasts, exposed and aroused, and then he lowered to focus on her apex where she glistened with her own juices. "Plump, velvety." Thanks be to the gods, soon he would bury himself there. "Wet."

He leaned forward and touched his mouth to her

instead. "Delicious," he spoke the word at her tight little opening. "So fucking delicious."

Addy was no longer Miss Adelaide Royal, schoolteacher, and spinster. She was his secret mistress, splayed out to be consumed by him as he pleased.

ADDY CLUTCHED the sides of his head to keep herself from turning into jelly, but also to keep him where she wanted him.

Trouble was, she wanted him everywhere.

He lifted her thighs onto his shoulder, accommodating his position and then claiming her again. His fingers were inside, while his mouth and jaw moved outside of her.

This friction. This heat.

Addy wanted more of him. She wanted the scratching and filling everywhere. She wanted him to stroke her, to plunge himself inside of her. She arched her back and squirmed. More.

More.

Yes.

"God, Adelaide." He slapped the side of her thigh.

And she even liked *that*.

A surge of sweet agony swept through her.

She was not the woman she'd believed herself to be.

"Let go, Adelaide." His voice rumbled from between her legs. And then every last sensation culminated into a white-hot explosion that rolled through, an all-consuming wave.

She stiffened, she reached, and then shuddered as shocks of pleasure pulsed through her veins.

Seconds—minutes?—later, her breathing slowed to normal.

The gradual awareness of his hair on her skin proved it had been real. Addy squeezed her eyes together and memorized the sensation of his chest between her knees. She would never, as long as she lived, forget what it felt like to have Damien Reddington kneeling before her.

"It isn't fair," she broke the silence causing him to glance up at her.

Seeing his mouth swollen and wet she nearly forgot what she was going to say.

"What isn't fair?"

"You've given me all the pleasure." She was not naïve. She realized what was required for the male to find completion in the act.

But they'd not performed the act.

That slow, slightly crooked grin stretched his mouth. "I've been wanting to savor you like that..." He paused as though calculating a mathematical problem of great significance. "Since Tuesday afternoon of Hardwood's wedding week. The maids brought in three trays of pastries and tea —*chocolate-filled* pastries and tea. Your eyes lit up, and your cheeks turned pink. The second you took your first bite of that scone I imagined doing this."

"Oh." Addy wasn't sure if she should be embarrassed by that or offended.

"That was the first time I imagined this scenario. The second was when dessert was served Wednesday night—"

"Those were the best treacle tarts I've ever had." She remembered them clearly. "They dissolved the second they landed on my tongue."

She exhaled wistfully at the memory and then realized he was still staring at her.

And she was still sprawled wantonly on the bench before him.

If a person was ever going to die of embarrassment, now would be her time.

And yet, oddly enough, she wasn't.

Not with him. Never with him.

She'd believed his attraction had been compelled by their proximity, by their circumstances.

But he'd just confessed to wanting to savor her *weeks ago*.

Before he'd been corralled into promising to escort her.

Before the Gazette's announcement.

And before Primm had practically demanded he take full responsibility of her.

"So… you liked doing that?"

He lifted one brow, nodding. "More than treacle tarts."

Well.

But what did it mean? What did it mean for his future? For his backup plan?

Damien lowered and then smoothed her skirts while Addy adjusted her bodice. A myriad of questions spinning in her brain, she couldn't help but notice how his breeches tented out.

He may have enjoyed savoring her, but at some point she wondered if she'd ever have the opportunity to reciprocate in some way.

And to keep herself from imagining what that would entail, she turned her thoughts back to desserts.

"Do you know what I miss most about America?" she asked.

Damien had made himself comfortable beside her again, and this time he drew her to recline against his side. "What do you miss the most?"

"There is the most glorious dessert—so glorious that it is, in fact, named the Knickerbocker Glory."

"And what makes the Knickerbocker Glory so wonderful?"

"It's put together in a tall glass—layers of iced cream, nuts, fruit, sweet bread, chocolate, topped off with whipped cream and a cherry on top. It's just... the most decadent thing in the world. I've never found anything like it in England and when I asked the cook at Primm's about it she looked at me as though I'd just suggested eating sugar straight from the larder."

"Hmmm..." he sounded tired. "It does sound a bit over-the-top." His chest rumbled behind her.

"Oh, but that's what makes it so absolutely magnificent." It reminded her of something.

She blinked as realization dawned.

It was almost as good as being savored.

And lucky for her, she didn't have to travel all the way to America for that.

HIS MOTHER

$\mathcal{D}$amien moved back and forth from a reserved affection to cool politeness.

He kept a polite distance when Coachman John was present, or when they'd checked into an inn for the night. And although he referred to her as Mrs. Reddington, he treated her with an almost cool respect.

She might even have felt slighted when Damien purchased separate chambers, but on the way up the stairs, he pulled her aside to explain that she'd want to be well-rested to meet with his mother the following day.

"And if I'm in your bed, Mrs. Reddington," he whispered when he stopped outside the door, "I couldn't promise that."

She'd been shocked and then pleased, and by the time he'd disappeared to help Coachman John, his explanation gave root to entirely different worries.

Tomorrow she would meet his mother.

If the Gazette had made its way to the school, it surely will have made its way to Reddington Park.

Most people, it seemed, were inclined to believe what

they read. So it was fair to assume Lady Bloodstone would assume they were married.

Even so, if Damien told his mother the truth of their marital status, what would she think of the circumstances in which they'd traveled since leaving London?

There was his sister to consider—an impressionable young girl on the cusp of womanhood.

"What are we going to tell your family once we've arrived?" It was the first subject she brought up when they took to the road the next day.

"What do you mean?"

Over the course of their short stay at Longbow Castle, Victoria had complained that the Earl, although a gentleman of great intelligence, could, at times, be endearingly clueless and Addy hadn't understood.

But staring at Damien now, she did.

"How do you intend to introduce me? As a teacher? As a governess?"

His brows rose and then he tilted his head to one side. "As my viscountess."

Addy glanced down at her hand, where her fingers intertwined with his.

He was treating this as though it was not a decision of major importance. And yet Addy knew that whatever they decided upon could very well determine the rest of their lives.

If he introduced her as his wife, he'd have no choice but to marry her. If he introduced her as a governess for his sister, they could not carry on as they'd been doing.

And then there was the announcement in the newspaper to consider.

"But what about your backup plan?"

ANNABELLE ANDERS

His frown crossed his expression so quickly that she almost missed it.

"I don't need it."

"You can't know that. Damien, we should come up with something else..." She hadn't figured that out just yet, but she'd never forgive herself if his estate fell into disrepair all because marrying her had sabotaged his backup plan.

"My ale is second to none," he boasted. "The recipe is solid. I have distributors in place who already have pubs eager to buy, and on top of all that, I employ loyal workers. It'll be fine, Adelaide. I needed a backup plan before, but now... I think it's time to let go of it."

Was he trying to convince her or himself?

"But—"

"As soon as we arrive, I'll arrange for a special license. It might be a little tricky, however, as we'll have to be discreet."

Because if they were already married, why would they need to marry again?

Addy drew in a deep breath. So it was decided. They would marry.

Was she prepared to take vows that would tie her to one man forever?

Everything had happened quickly—too quickly. But what choice did they really have?

She stared down at their hands again. If he was convinced they could weather this, then fighting it would just make everything more difficult.

In the short run.

As far as the long run, that remained to be seen.

***

No more back-up plan. The notion of falling back on some chit's dowry in case his brewery failed was now officially up in smoke.

His gut twisted as they made the last turn leading to his estate.

Reddington Park. The place that was his home, the place that represented a legacy that went back over four hundred years.

But pride wasn't the only thing that twisted his gut. At least half the twisting was from the massive responsibility that came with it.

Revenue from rents had failed to keep them in the black since his father's reign. They could not continue in that direction.

The brewery would be a success. And a massive one at that.

It had to be.

But if he didn't remedy the circumstances set up by the Gazette's announcement, he'd have to sacrifice his honor.

And what good was all of this if he lost his honor?

"It's breathtaking," Addy was leaning forward as she took in the vast structure that was his. Peering outside from beside her, Damien imagined it through her eyes.

With crumbling turrets at each end flanking a patchwork tower, the core dated back to the Norman invasion. The more usable parts of the structure hadn't been built until four centuries later.

"Most of the brewing takes place in the tower. Water is pumped from the lake up to the brew kettles where it's heated and where the mashing takes place." He'd told her all of this before.

"And then it travels in pipes to the lower floors? Right? So it can be stored in the cellars."

Damien nodded. She was a good listener.

He bit back a grin. "My father appreciated the irony of brewing ale in a tower built for prayer."

"It was once a nunnery." Addy confirmed.

Damien nodded. "You can stumble across a few interesting chambers when you get away from the main parts of the house—from the modern wings."

The entire manor, really, was a bit of a hodgepodge.

A hodgepodge that had, however, stood the test of time. God help him, he wouldn't be the viscount who failed it.

"There is nothing remotely as old as this in America." She glanced over at him. "I love imagining all the goings-on over hundreds and hundreds of years. Every summer break since I began to teach, I made a point to tour at least one of the nearby estates. If the owners are away, that is." She twisted around to watch the scenery again.

"Hardwood's father hated the practice—claimed that commoners had no business seeing how their betters lived." The former earl's nasty countenance was no secret. Damien shook his head. "But not my mother," he smiled. "Even though she resides here year-round, she allots several dates for guests to tour the public areas. Not the brewery, or the bedchambers and private suites, of course."

"Of course not." Addy glanced back at him again. "That is generous of her."

Damien nodded. Neither of his parents had ever lacked in generosity, sometimes to their own detriment.

"Oh! There are people standing outside."

"The servants are anxious to greet the new viscountess," Damien said, squinting his eyes. If he'd had any doubts before that the news of his 'marriage' had reached Reddington Park, the traditional inspection of the household put those firmly to rest.

Because he knew damn well it wasn't him they were waiting to see.

There was a new mistress of the house. And whether Addy was ready or not, that mistress was her.

***

Addy's heart lodged itself in her throat as Damien led her from the carriage to where meticulously uniformed servants stood in two perfectly straight lines.

But before they addressed the butler, a blond whirlwind came flying out to throw herself into Damien's arms.

"Dame!" The young girl had to be his sister, Caledonia.

"I haven't been gone all that long, Callie." But Damien squeezed the younger girl with equal fervor.

Just behind them, an older woman had been led outside by a maid.

But the elegant lady wasn't staring at them. She had her head tilted back and her eyes focused on nothing at all.

She was blind.

Damien's mother was blind.

"Mother." Damien extracted himself from his sister's exuberant embrace to cross to her.

"Aren't you a sight for sore eyes," the woman teased and Damien leaned down and kissed both her cheeks. "And I understand you have a bride with you?"

Not even a hint of sarcasm or criticism carried in her voice. In fact, when she turned her head in Addy's direction, her expression was one of pure welcome.

Addy froze, uncertain as to what to do. Such a reception was...

Unexpected.

"I do." Damien took his mother's arm and led her back to where Addy stood feeling terribly awkward. "Adelaide. May I present you to my mother, the Viscountess Bloodstone. Mother, I've brought home a wife, Adelaide, formerly Royal, now Reddington."

"The *Dowager* Viscountess, Damien dear." His mother turned her face in Addy's general direction. "And we are honored to meet you. May I call you Adelaide? And you must call me Sarah. We are family now."

Warmth began in Addy's chest, warming her heart unexpectedly.

Even her own aunt had never called her that.

Family.

"It's my pleasure to meet *you*, my lady." Addy could not call the viscountess by her given name. And then she understood where her son had learned how to provide comfort.

Lady Bloodstone reached out for Addy's hand and then drew her into a warm embrace. "We are so very happy Damien has found someone to marry. And we have so many questions! But first, you must settle in." She dropped her arms from around Addy and stepped backward. "I've had my chamber cleared out. It was time."

Her chamber? Oh no! Addy could not take the viscountess' chamber! She and Damien were not even really married.

Damien's sister welcomed Addy next. "You must call me Callie." It struck Addy that the girl was a feminine version of her brother, right down to the same violet eyes. "Did the school pass muster, then?" The girl twisted around to question Damien. "Am I to attend Miss Primm's this autumn?"

Damien frowned at this. "Plenty of time to discuss that later." He rubbed his hands together, and although he was obviously pleased to see his mother and sister, Addy sensed his urgency to dispense with the expected formalities so he could look in on his brewery.

He gestured for Addy to join him and then introduced her to the servants as Lady Bloodstone. The new viscountess.

"Welcome home, my lord. Welcome to Reddington Park, my lady." One by one, beginning with the more senior servants, she and Damien were greeted.

Caledonia and Lady Bloodstone followed quietly behind and then assured her she would not be expected to remember everyone's name. Their unwavering and joyful kindness nearly overwhelmed her, to be met with open arms at seemingly every turn. Addy could hardly believe her luck. Because...

Damien's family...

Was positively lovely.

With Damien in high demand and anxious to look in on his brewery operations, it was Lady Bloodstone and his sister who showed Addy to the master's apartment— divided into two suites. The viscountess' suite was comprised of not one room, but several: one with a tall, canopied bed, a second one made up as a private sitting room, and then doors leading to various dressing rooms. "For your lady's maid," the viscountess informed her.

"Oh, but I don't have one." And she never would. "I am a schoolteacher. I *was* a schoolteacher."

"But you are also the daughter of a very wealthy man."

Lady Bloodstone's smile was serene. "And now, you are a viscountess. I'll ask Molly to place an advertisement first thing tomorrow. And until you've decided on a candidate, I'll send up one of the chamber maids to assist you." Addy vaguely remembered Molly to be the housekeeper.

"Oh, but I—"

"And we've all the preliminary plans in place for a celebratory wedding ball! If I wasn't just so very happy he's finally married, I'd be angry with both of you for having a secret wedding. But we'll make up for it with a magnificent country celebration."

"That's not necess—"

"I know it's a little overwhelming now." Lady Bloodstone patted Addy's hand. "But important events such as weddings cannot go by without being acknowledged properly."

Another servant had entered carrying a tray. "Now here is Clara with tea for you. The bell pull is in the corner there if you need anything, but Callie and I will leave you alone to rest." She reached out one hand and her companion immediately took it. "We will talk more at dinner tonight."

"Thank you." All Addy could do was nod as her mother and sister-in-law left her alone in the luxurious chamber.

Overwhelmed was too small a word to describe her feelings.

Because sitting alone, in this magnificent chamber, in a veritable castle, being addressed as a viscountess, all her doubts returned.

WHAT DOWRY?

 uch later that night—following an elegant but intimate dinner—rather than retire right away, Damien retreated to his study.

Which always reminded him of his father.

Leaning back in the well-worn leather chair, he closed his eyes and inhaled the familiar cedar and spice that lingered in the room. His father had been gone for five years now, but in this room, seated at his father's desk, Damien never failed to feel an inkling of his father's presence.

The presence of a man who'd not always made the right choices, but had followed his heart.

And for the most part, had experienced success. His father had been…

Happy.

Damien sighed. Despite inheriting the repercussions of some of his father's poor decisions, he could not find it in his heart to resent him. His father had been born a viscount, but he'd also been very human—just as Damien himself was.

Not all of his father's decisions had been without merit; he had married well, he'd never missed a single vote in parliament, and as viscount, he not only treated his equals, but also his servants and employees, with all due respect.

And now, the endeavor his father had begun as a hobby, the brewery, was on the verge of thriving.

Every indication was that this batch would be the best yet. Orders were already coming in, and if he could juggle the revenues and expenditures just right, they'd be turning a profit by this time next year.

"Darling? Are you in here?" His mother's voice interrupted his thoughts. He dropped his feet to the floor and leaned forward.

"I am." He crossed the room and she dismissed her companion. She was capable of finding the chair on her own, but Damien led her to it anyway.

He was well aware of his mother's delight at being doted upon.

"It's been a very long day, has it not?" She folded her hands in her lap, knees together and looking perfectly proper. "Oh, but I do like Adelaide. When I first learned of your abrupt marriage, and that she was American, I'll admit to having been concerned. But I trust your judgment completely. And now that I've met her, I see why you didn't want to let her get away."

This came as no surprise to Damien. Adelaide, his mother, and his sister had gotten along swimmingly at dinner. They'd taken to her better than he ever could have hoped for.

His mother smiled and blinked slowly. "Furthermore, and most important of all, I sense that you have great affection for her. And that makes me happier than you can ever know."

But this was the difficult part—lying to his own mother. "I'm glad."

His mother was not easily fooled and had been doing this for as long as he could remember. *Reading him.* Guessing at his thoughts before he could think them himself.

"It's in your voice. I've never heard you address any other lady with that tone."

Her words gave him pause. She was not wrong. Trouble was, he hadn't sorted his feelings for Adelaide out yet. How could this be a matter of the heart when they'd both been forced into it?

At the very least, he desired her. It was as good a place to begin as any.

Even now, a battle waged within. Adelaide was upstairs in their shared chambers.

Was she waiting for him to come to her? Was that something she would want tonight?

They'd been together intimately, but he had not, in fact, made love to her.

Should he wait until the marriage was legal?

"And you are happy," she added. "As am I! Because now I can begin imagining myself a grandmother. But first things first. As soon as Callie read me the announcement, we began planning a wedding ball for you and Adelaide. Just because your ceremony was a private one, doesn't mean we'll have to celebrate in private. Which is why I'm here."

A wedding ball—one that would no doubt cost a fortune.

"What can I do for you, Mother?"

"I require Adelaide's father's address."

Mr. Charles Royal.

At the very least, Damien would be honest with her about this.

"I've not met with him, Mother. There is no contract, and it's doubtful there will be a dowry."

But his mother was shaking her head. "You haven't seen it yet, then. A very thick package arrived via special messenger yesterday. Pitkins told me the return address is Royal Enterprises—your father-in-law's company. Naturally, I wouldn't attempt to read something addressed to you," she teased. "But I imagine it contains a marriage contract."

"Naturally." Damien frowned, curious as to what Adelaide's father had to say about the announcement.

Knowing of the man's reputation, Damien would either be invited to meet the man at dawn, or pay some sort of penalty for the privilege of marrying his daughter. The Mad American Royal hadn't achieved his nickname for no reason.

Damien shot his gaze to the stack of unopened letters and located it easily enough.

Unwilling to put it off, he broke the wax seal and opened it up.

Inside, he found a thick set of papers titled *"Marriage Contract"*. Folded in the contract, a note from the Royal Bank of England.

Adelaide, no doubt, would appreciate the irony of that.

He blinked at the hastily scrawled script, however, hoping that by some miracle the man had changed his mind. But Addy had been right.

The amount that jumped out at him had his heart sinking into his boots.

One hundred pounds.

At the bottom a postscript read, *"Adelaide's dowry"*.

One hundred pounds.

To a schoolteacher, it was a year's worth of wages. In the grand scheme of running a viscountcy, it was a pittance. His backup plan was no more.

"We are not so isolated up here so that we have not heard of Miss Royal's father's antics. But he has sent a dowry after all, has he not?" His mother's words pushed him into a corner.

"He has." Charles Royal had a cruel sense of humor.

And yet, Damien also found an odd sense of peace in knowing he had her father's permission.

If not any of the man's money.

Perhaps it was a sign from his own father—to follow his heart. To believe in himself.

Or was it to uphold the Reddington honor first and deal with the aftermath later?

Damien folded the note quietly, not wishing to alert his mother to anything amiss.

"I knew there would be. And you needn't worry about Adelaide's wardrobe as I've sent for a modiste to come right away. She must be beautiful to have attracted my son, but Callie said her gowns are a little outdated. You of all people know that a little polish goes a long way. People will have certain expectations of her. So along with a gown for the ball, we'll begin working on an entirely new wardrobe." With that taken care of, his mother rose and brushed her hands together.

"But you must be tired. Lead me to the door, darling, and I'll leave you to your business. But don't leave dearest Addy alone too long. Newlyweds have certain expectations as well…" Her mouth curved into a teasing smile.

"I love you, Mother, but I'm disinclined to discuss that aspect of marriage with you, now or ever." He led her to the door where her companion awaited her outside, and after dutifully kissing his mother's cheek, he wished her goodnight.

Back in his study, he marched across the room and lifted the note from Royal off the desk.

The man's handwriting was barely legible, making it nearly impossible for Damien to decipher the details.

But the message was clear.

Marrying Adelaide Royal would not result in a fortune for him or anyone else. He'd known this all along.

Damien marched across to the hearth and threw it into the fire.

He had a warm and willing woman awaiting him upstairs.

He'd address the details tomorrow.

HER NOT-QUITE HUSBAND

"Come in," Addy's heart skipped a beat when a knock sounded from the adjoining door.

And then it skipped another at the sight of Damien.

Her not-quite husband.

Standing in the threshold, in shirtsleeves and barefooted, his demeanor was that of indecision.

He did not feign some cheerful greeting. Nor did he make excuses for his presence.

"I'll go, if you want me to."

It meant he had been thinking along the same lines that she was.

Everyone thought they were married anyway...

"The lines have been blurred, have they not?" Addy said. But before he misconstrued her answer, she added, "Don't go."

Addy had missed him.

He closed the door that adjoined their two suites, and for the first time since she'd known Damien Reddington, he appeared...

Nervous?

"I like your family," Addy announced, wanting to fill in the sudden silence. "Very much."

He nodded but then glanced toward the seating area, where her book was splayed face down on the table. "You aren't reading ahead without me, are you?"

"Just a few pages." She shifted her gaze back to him. "Did you come here so we could read together?"

He flashed a quick grin. "I'll admit that's not what I had in mind."

But then that indecision returned as he lowered himself onto the settee.

"I received a letter from your father. It includes a marriage contract, and..." His gaze shot to the fire. He stilled as though entranced by the flames, but when he turned back to her, he looked as though he'd come to some sort of decision.

"What is it?" Addy asked.

"He included payment of your dowry."

This was the very last news Addy expected.

"My dowry?" She could hardly believe her ears. "My father sent you my dowry?" But this was wonderful news! It meant that Damien no longer required a back-up plan.

Because he had her!

And it also meant that she wouldn't be a burden. She'd have something to contribute to her new family.

"You are saying that my father paid you my dowry?"

"Directly from the Royal Bank of London." He reached across and took her hand. "So you needn't worry, Adelaide."

"And neither do you!" She burst out of her chair, truly happy for the first time in what felt like weeks. Yes, it was true that she and Damien had not really worked out all the details of their relationship, but aside from the fact that neither had felt they'd had a choice, their greatest obstacle had been her lack of a dowry.

Hadn't it?

"Now you can make all the improvements necessary to your brewery, and to the manor and your tenant living conditions." And she could send Primm some money for the school.

Addy would not hold a grudge. Primm was only doing what was best for the school.

Damien was shaking his head. "Eventually. Yes," he said. How could he look so calm in the face of their good luck? Perhaps he was in shock.

"My father isn't such a villain after all, is he?" She'd always suspected that deep down her father loved her. This only proved it. "He loves me," she smiled. "I knew it."

"Of course he loves you. How could he not?" Damien hadn't moved but simply watched her.

"Oh, but this makes me so happy! You don't need to find a lady to marry for your backup plan," she was practically gushing in her relief. "You have me!" And unable to help herself, she took him by the hands and tugged him out of the chair.

She was no longer a burden, no longer a problem, Addy's confidence emboldened her to gaze at him with all the adoration she'd been wanting to show.

He wasn't quite her husband, not yet—but that didn't matter.

"You have me, Damien. Now what are you going to do with me?" She felt like a bride on her wedding night.

He'd said that he'd only begun to teach her all the ways they could bring one another pleasure. Addy hadn't allowed herself to believe they would have time for her to learn them all.

But suddenly those doubts were nowhere to be found.

Not only did his mother seem to genuinely welcome her, and his sister, and the servants. But she brought with her the money to build onto his family's legacy.

A legacy that would also be hers.

Because...

She was *family*.

"What am I going to do with you?" Damien repeated her question. And then, as though having come to a very important decision, he swooped her into his arms and carried her to the bed. "You'll find out soon enough."

*D*amien situated Adelaide on the bed and stepped back. "Aren't you going to join me?" she teased.

Her full lips tilted up at the corners. She lounged back on her elbows, golden-red curls falling back, and bent one knee.

"Patience, my sweet Adelaide." Reluctant to have her out of his sight, he drew his shirt over his head and then devoured her with his gaze. He was, in fact, the impatient one.

Even though he didn't deserve her.

But she was staring at him with greedy eyes and the air charged around them as though the entire universe had schemed for this moment.

She wore nothing but a lightweight night rail—one he'd dispense with soon enough—but it revealed her soft curves, the swell of her breasts and hips, and the indent of her waist. Her delicate feet peeked out from beneath the hem.

Blood rushed to his groin. As he fumbled at the fasteners

of his falls, he pushed away the pricking at the back of his neck.

Damien had fully intended to reveal the amount her father had sent. It had been on the tip of his tongue to tell her.

But then she'd burst off the settee, with a smile that lit up the room. How could he take that from her?

She'd agreed to marry him without the dowry but she'd been reluctant. She'd not wanted to be a burden. Believing she was bringing funds to their union would squash those doubts.

The final straw, however, had landed when she'd spoken of her father—when she'd believed that her father had not forgotten her after all—that he'd cared.

That he'd loved her all along.

The withdrawal of her dowry made sense if her father's actions had come from some hidden agenda designed to weed out unsuitable husbands.

Damien couldn't take that away.

As long as the brewery succeeded, she need never know.

"You are happy?" She bit her lip, his pause giving her concern.

"I am if you are." His breeches unfastened, he took one step toward the bed. "You're sure?"

She nodded. "So very sure," and then she grinned. "Everyone thinks we're—"

"—married anyway," he finished for her.

They stared at one another in the candlelight, grinning like fools.

This was right. They would make this work.

Not taking the time to step out of his breeches, Damien

surged onto the bed, covering her, sinking her into the mattress, and claiming her mouth at the same time.

"God's breath, Addy. I've waited too long for this." He gripped her thighs even as she locked her feet around his hips.

"I can't believe this is happening." She arched her back, giving him better access to her throat.

She was perfect.

This was perfect. *Almost.*

Her happy.

That was all he wanted in the world.

Damien dismissed the misgivings that threatened to ruin the moment. She wanted kisses; he'd drown her in them. She wanted carnal pleasure; he'd die providing them. "I've wanted it since I met you. I've wanted you since I met you."

With their breath mingling, she clasped her hands along his face. "You don't have to say that."

"I know."

Damien moved his hips in a slow circle, creating more friction between them and making sure she comprehended just how badly he'd wanted her. "I didn't want to want you. But instead of going away, it grew stronger. It got even worse when I realized you seemed to be doing your clever best to avoid me."

"Only because you made me feel so nervous."

"Are you nervous now?" He needed to get her out of this night rail, and himself out of his breeches.

Addy's hands smoothed down his bare chest. "I am—a little. But you know what to do, right?"

Something between a laugh and a choke bubbled up his throat. "I believe I do."

He'd always imagined schoolteachers and bluestockings to be starchy and uptight. Addy...

Was just the opposite. She was soft and willing and simply...

Addy.

The woman he'd make his wife.

Kissing her filled him up even as it detonated other needs. She wiggled beneath him, assisting him at removing her gown and lowering his breeches. Nestling between her thighs again, he was rewarded with the most delicate flesh.

Drown in her. The words compelled Damien to submerge himself in the sensation of Adelaide—to inhale her sweet scent, to taste warm vanilla breath, to stroke silken skin.

He poised himself at her entrance. *Drown in her.*

And yes, to bury himself in her tight, velvety sheath.

He hovered, his cock at her opening, and stared into her eyes. "I'm here."

She nodded.

Heart racing, muscles shaking, Damien inched forward as the anticipation of this moment came to fruition. He required all his self-control to move slowly, carefully.

As he claimed her body, he lost his soul in her gaze.

Adelaide's mouth parted, tiny breaths trembled past her lips.

She held none of her emotions back.

Any unease she had turned to wonder, and then to delight. She was not a passive participant. Once he was seated to the hilt, her intimate muscles clenched around him. He withdrew and her eyes darkened, and when he thrust again, she met his force with a thrust of her own. She squeezed him and writhed, pumping him for more pleasure as though she'd been doing this all her life.

It was good. Two people becoming one. This was good.

And not only was she eager, but his not-quite wife was insatiable.

He'd barely dozed off when her hands teased at him again. To reward her inquisitive courage, he flipped her onto her belly and taken her from behind.

Just before dawn, they made love a third time, slowly while facing one another, each lying on their sides.

"It's not too much?" He'd asked, hooking her leg over his waist.

"Not too much." She'd pressed forward and he'd moved in and out of her. With their gazes locked, they worked together, unfolding their passion until neither could hold back.

And as the sun crept over the horizon and into the room, she cuddled against him, not caring that their sweat mingled, or that he remained half inside her body. "It's as if we're already married, isn't it?"

Her words prodded his last semblance of regret. Because she was right.

Long after Addy drifted off to sleep, Damien stared at the ceiling from beside her. From this point forward, he was well and truly committed.

Success was no longer an option. He turned his mind to the brewery and all the possible scenarios that would increase profits.

Because he not only had an estate, his mother and sister to provide for. He also had a wife.

And there was no going back. Damien was once and for all, undoubtably, without a backup plan.

THE GUEST OF HONOR

*O*btaining the special license wasn't as simple as Damien had expected it to be.

The day following their arrival, as he was making to leave to meet with the local bishop, the influx of a handful of distant relatives effectively nixed his outing. But one day's delay wouldn't hurt, he rationalized. Aside from explaining the necessity of his errand, his mother made it perfectly clear that she expected he and Adelaide to act the proper host and hostess.

It didn't matter that they had not done the inviting.

And as days passed, yet more guests arrived, including both of his mother's sisters, his father's aunt, and several distant cousins. But of course, they required both Damien and Adelaide's attention.

And by the end of one full week, when he finally thought he could make a successful getaway, it was his brewery master who managed to thwart him. He had questions regarding some of the machinery that needed to be repaired as well as some of the bricks in one of the chimneys that needed replacing.

Both of which were rather urgent.

Each night, when Damien told Addy that they'd have to put their secret wedding off again, she'd been understanding.

"Tomorrow I'll leave first thing in the morning," he vowed while lying in bed after being frustrated yet again. With the elaborate ball set to take place in less than a fortnight, the house had fallen into a state of organized chaos.

"I'm not worried," Addy pressed a kiss along his jaw. "It doesn't really matter, does it? It's not as though you're going to jilt me." Her voice was breezy, but Damien knew her well enough to recognize hidden doubts.

"Never," he rolled to face her. But his words didn't chase the uncertainty out of her eyes. Before they'd arrived at Reddington Park, the fact that she lacked a dowry had hovered like a dark cloud between them.

Now, another cloud seemed to be gathering.

Had he made a mistake when he'd lied to her about the amount her father sent? But no. He couldn't take her father's love away.

The clouds would pass. Of course they would.

***

As welcoming as Lady Bloodstone and Callie had been, Addy experienced a true sense of home upon the arrival of another former teacher from Miss Primm's.

Miss Priscilla Fellowes—now Lady Hardwood—returned from her honeymoon in France filled with marital contentment.

Lord Hardwood's estate bordered Reddington Park, and it was at their wedding that Addy had originally met Damien.

"I didn't expect to see you again for months!" Priscilla tucked her hand in Addy's arm when they strolled through the garden. "And I am beyond thrilled to have you for a neighbor."

"None of this was expected," Addy admitted, and then, not wanting to perpetuate more lies with her friend, changed the subject. "How do you find married life?"

Priscilla's mouth stretched into a satisfied smile. "I could not be happier. I'm coming to believe that I knew Emerson was my special person from the first moment we met."

"Was that when he dove into the lake to save Fiddlesticks?"

How could any of them forget? The pup had fallen through the ice in the middle of winter and would have perished if not for Lord Hardwood's quick thinking and heroic actions. Priscilla had returned to the school to share the harrowing tale in which one of their students'+ dogs had nearly met with tragedy.

"He wasn't only handsome, but there was something... something else..." Priscilla squeezed Addy's arm. "But you know the feeling. You must or you wouldn't have married so quickly. Was Primm terribly disappointed about losing another teacher? I haven't had the chance to write her since I've been back."

Addy had been debating within herself how much of the truth to share with Priscilla, but at this turn of the conversation, she decided she needed a confidante.

She hated fooling Damien's mother and sister. Her

happiness with Damien felt tarnished until her marriage was a real one.

"We aren't married," Addy blurted out. "It was a mistake."

And then she went on to tell Priscilla an abbreviated version of everything that had occurred since the day of Chloe and Captain Edgeworth's wedding.

Well, not quite *everything*.

But, listening intently, Priscilla strolled silently for nearly a minute before turning to Addy with a frown. "Primm sacked you?"

"She didn't have a choice, really."

"It seems awfully harsh… But I suppose the point is a moot one." Priscilla resumed strolling. "And you've decided to marry him anyway. I must admit I'm disappointed to hear that this wasn't some serendipitous romance that began the week of my wedding," she half-joked. "Are you certain this isn't also a love-match? I saw the way Bloodstone looked at you and it was uncannily similar to looks I receive from Hardwood."

Addy dropped her gaze to the grass. "There is some… affection between the two of us. And we have been…" Addy rolled her lips together before adding, "living as man and wife."

Silence, but for the leaves rustling in the breeze, followed her declaration.

"You mean—"

"Yes." Addy did not meet Priscilla's gaze. "I think this spot calls for sunflowers. What do you think?"

But Priscilla wasn't yet prepared to abandon this conversation.

"The dowry from your father notwithstanding, it doesn't

ensure your protection until you're legally married. When is the ceremony, Addy? What is Bloodstone waiting for?"

Addy explained the difficulties Damien had experienced in getting away to meet with the bishop, the demands of his mother and the brewery—but that it would happen soon.

"This cannot continue." Priscilla was practically marching now. "Hardwood can make the trip into town with your... *husband* to obtain the special license. As for the ceremony, that can take place the day after the ball. We'll tell Lady Bloodstone that we're all going on a picnic together. Emerson and I can be your witnesses. You cannot go on with matters up in the air like this, Addy."

"We won't." Addy said. Damien was as frustrated by all of this as she'd been. It wasn't as though he'd put it off by choice.

Even so, it was reassuring to have Priscilla as an advocate.

"Do you love him?" Priscilla finally asked.

Addy had expected this question. Because Priscilla, more than anyone of her acquaintance, understood that one could not pick and choose their person to love.

"With all my heart," Addy answered. "And it's terrifying." Because as relieved as she'd been to learn that her father had provided her with a dowry, it meant she would never know if she'd have been good enough to be Damien's wife without it.

"Love does not come without risks," Priscilla said. "But the rewards are worth every one of them."

"I hope you're right, Priscilla. I hope you're right."

***

The remainder of the afternoon following Priscilla's visit proved as busy and chaotic as Addy had come to expect.

Lady Bloodstone might very well lack the ability to see, but she made up for that with an unerring sense of purpose and organization. She had gathered not only her contemporaries in the neighborhood but several young women from the village so that no detail was left to chance. Details such as tying ribbons, arranging flowers, and a myriad of other tasks had been undertaken as needed. Other help came in the form of all of Lord Hardwood's sisters and his mother, along with dozens of unfamiliar faces Addy hoped to one day become acquainted with.

But Addy had been excused from having to participate in most of these preparations. As the guest of honor—as the *viscount's new bride*—Addy's primary responsibility was limited to not much more than sitting for a local hair stylist, and enduring the final fittings for her dress that was being made especially for the ball.

It was the arrival of that gown that startled Addy into the reality of all of it.

Made up of an emerald gossamer silk, the material flowed like a cloud from where it was cinched at Addy's waist with jeweled buttons. Delicately sewn lace lined the fitted bodice, which drew attention to her décolletage without seeming immodest.

Never in all her seven and twenty years had Addy imagined herself wearing such a gown.

And she was the guest of honor. Not her father, not her aunt, nor even one of her students.

In the eyes of the world, Adelaide was already Damien's viscountess—his wife.

And the morning after the ball, it would be made legal.
She was going to be *Lady Bloodstone*.

LADY BLOODSTONE

"Oh, my lady. You look like a princess." Diana, Addy's newly hired lady's maid, fastened the last button and then turned Addy to face the looking glass.

It was as though Addy was staring at a stranger. And it was not only the perfectly fitted gown of the latest fashion that transformed her so, nor was it her hair, which had been expertly styled and adorned with jewels.

It was something more intangible than anything so mundane—a look in her eyes—a glow that brightened her cheeks.

Before leaving that morning to meet with Hardwood, Damien had taken his time making love with her.

He'd said he required sustenance if he was going to be away from her all day.

Even hours later, the image of him gazing down at her, moving in and out of her and calling her *my love,* warmed her blood.

So when she stared into the looking glass, she did not

see a tentative schoolteacher, nor a young woman who'd been ousted by the ton.

She saw a confident woman. She saw a woman newly awakened to her own sensuality and capable of taking on the world.

She saw herself looking like someone she'd only ever dreamed of.

A knock sounded on the door from the adjoining suite, and her heart jumped.

"Come in." Her voice only shook a little.

How many times had her knees gone weak at the sight of him? Damien stepped inside, dressed in what could only be described as wedding finery.

Would she really marry this beautiful man?

He stepped closer and she caught a hint of his cologne. His hair had been combed away from his face in a manner that made him appear slightly roguish, but his cravat was tied into an elaborate bow; jewels adorned the lace at his wrists, and the crocheted designs on his waistcoat may very well have been spun from gold.

But none of that compared to his eyes, or to the look of awe transforming his expression.

"You look..." her voice caught. Did ladies call their husbands beautiful?

"You look beautiful," he spoke over her. "My God, Adelaide." He closed the distance between them. Taking her hands in his, he extended one leg and executed a perfect bow.

It was the perfect moment.

Addy could die tomorrow, and this moment would have ensured she'd lived her life to the fullest.

And when she met his gaze, he sent her a slow wink.

A wink that reminded her of their time together earlier that morning. A wink which was meant to encourage her for the night ahead.

But also a wink which suggested to her that he'd successfully secured the license.

"Are we to go ahead with our picnic with Lord and Lady Hardwood tomorrow?" she asked, feeling coy. Because she could not ask him outright with Diana in the room.

He dipped his chin and Addy exhaled.

One more night and then this particular aspect of their deception would be over.

Their marriage would be real.

She only wished she could reconcile the feelings she had about her dowry. On one hand, she was infinitely grateful that Damien needn't worry over finances well into the future. On the other hand, the very existence of the dowry meant she'd never know...

Would she have been good enough for him without it? Would his mother and sister and all the guests coming to the ball that evening have accepted her the same if her dowry had been, perhaps, only ten thousand pounds?

"Your mother asked that we meet her in the drawing room at a quarter before the hour." Addy forced her thoughts away from matters which she had no control over.

Because she *did* feel beautiful.

She *did* feel special.

"Then we'd best make our way down." Damien reached out, and she slid her hand along his arm, allowing him to lead her into the corridor.

"Did you have luck today?" Addy whispered, keeping her words vague because, although this section of the hall was empty, one could never be certain no servants were lurking about.

"Indeed. The bishop is expecting us first thing in the morning." Damien slid her a sideways glance. "You aren't going to jilt me, are you?"

Was there a hint of vulnerability in the question? Her heart twisted.

"Of course not." And then she lowered her voice further. "But you must sleep in your chamber tonight. I cannot think sharing a bed on our wedding eve would bring anything but bad luck."

"I hadn't realized there were any such legends that would determine our sleeping arrangements."

"I don't think there are, but…" Addy sent him a mock scowl. "Perhaps there ought to be."

"So my bed will remain cold tonight because of a legend that ought to be. I ought to have realized how superstitious you were when you threw the flowers."

"You threw the coins," she reminded him.

"To keep them from following us all the way to Mayfair."

But then Damien slid his arm around her waist and lowered his mouth to her ear. "I wouldn't have you any other way," he whispered.

There wasn't time to further discuss the intricacies of wedding rituals and superstitions as they'd arrived at the formal withdrawing room where Damien's mother, Callie, and a few other relatives awaited them.

Addy straightened her back even as Damien released her and did the same. Stepping inside to greet Damien's family, she put on a welcoming smile and took her position among her future family.

Shortly after, she stood beside Damien, the two of them

accepting congratulation upon congratulation as an endless line of guests made their way through the foyer and into the ballroom.

Damien managed to touch her elbow when she most needed the connection and he caught her eye whenever she needed a bolster of strength.

And as she and Damien's family entered the ballroom, Addy held her head high when the major domo introduced her as the Viscountess Bloodstone.

Candlelight danced from the chandeliers above, flowers provided a delicate fragrance, and the champagne flowed freely, sparkling as toast after toast was raised.

Even the first dance, a waltz, went off without so much as a hiccup. How could it not when she was accompanied by Damien Reddington?

Envy twisted a few of the ladies' stares, and there were a few jealous whispers, but mostly there were romantic sighs.

And it *was* rather romantic—a viscount marrying a schoolteacher.

She might have exhaled a few romantic sighs of her own, being on the receiving end of Damien's loving glances... his charm.

As to speculation of a love match, Addy might never know for certain.

But how could she not love him? How could she not acknowledge herself to be one of the luckiest ladies in all of London?

Addy was accepted here.

Addy was going to have the family she'd always wanted.

And somehow, everything was perfect despite it all being a farce.

By the time supper was served, Addy had decided—with

a little help from the champagne—that she was going to be happy here.

"I imagine your students are going to miss you dreadfully," one of Damien's cousins offered.

Now that Addy was sitting, all the dancing and mingling caught up with her. "I will miss them," she answered, mildly distracted at the sight of her husband—*her future husband*—procuring her a plate at the buffet.

Without a doubt, Damien was the most handsome man in attendance. Even following hours of dancing, an energy surrounded him as he moved from one group to another, never allowing more than half an hour to pass without searching her out from across the room.

Her breath caught as she gazed upon him now, at the way he appeared to almost glow.

The embroidery on his waistcoat sparkled, and candlelight caught glints of gold in his hair.

But there was no amount of radiance to rival his essence.

He turned and caught her watching him. And from across the dance floor, the smirk of promise in his smoldering look sent intimate tingles dancing down her spine.

Addy licked her lips. Perhaps it wouldn't be bad luck to share her bed with him tonight. Why bow to a silly foreboding when she could be joined with the man who'd owned her heart and soul?

Would it be so very bad to wake up on the morning of their wedding with him beside her?

But just as that thought flickered, murmurs seemed to roll through the room like a wave. And then shouts rose up. "Fire!"

Guests began moving toward the exits, and this time,

when Addy found Damien's face, he was rushing toward her with fierce determination in his eyes.

"Fire?"

As though to give credence to the warning, a hint of smoke wafted near the ceiling.

And in the next instant, bedlam broke loose.

RUNNING TOWARD DANGER

*D*amien's first instinct was to get to Adelaide—to ensure that she, his mother, and his sister got to safety.

But he also had the well-being of two-hundred ballroom guests to secure.

Because regardless of where the fire had started, or how, it was ultimately his responsibility to ensure no one was hurt.

Nonetheless, he pulled Addy into his arms. "Where is—"

"Your mother is with your sister." Addy supplied, looking up at him. "I'll make sure they get outside. Hopefully, it's only a simple kitchen fire, but we'll need to organize a brigade."

This petite princess of a woman was all efficiency. Damien squeezed her shoulders and pressed his mouth to hers for a strengthening kiss—as much for himself as it was for her.

"Pitkins will order them all outside to the fountain in the garden." If this fire hadn't originated in the kitchen, he

244

suspected it was one of the exposed chimneys in the tower. The image of the crumbling bricks in the southwest chimney flashed in his mind. And then his thoughts jumped to his mother, shrouded in the dark of her blindness. "You'll stay with her?"

"I'll find her now. Go, Damien." But as he went to step back, she reached out and caught his arm. Concern transformed her expression. "Be careful. Don't do anything foolish."

His heart skipped a beat. She was one small woman. "Keep outside, Addy. I need to know you're safe." As long as he knew she was out of harm's way he could focus on what needed done.

Somehow, she'd become... everything. But the smoke was thickening.

And it wasn't coming from the kitchens.

"I will! I promise!" She squeezed his arm and then looking as though she was going to say something, but changing her mind, released it. "Go."

Damien nodded, torn for an instant, and then sprinted out of the ballroom.

He did not run in the direction of safety, however, but to where the smoke was thick.

Damien ran toward the fire.

***

Addy stood a safe distance away, in the gazebo on the hill behind the house. She held Lady Bloodstone's arm on one side and Caledonia was on the other. They, along with a crowd of their guests, stared down at the fire licking at the sky.

It had begun in the tower rising up from the center of the manor—the chamber where Damien brewed his ale.

Where he no doubt fought valiantly that very moment.

Please, God, protect him.

He'd promised not to be foolish, but she couldn't count on that.

He was a man, after all.

"Is it spreading?" Damien's mother held her face in the direction of the house.

"I don't think so," Addy answered. "But it's difficult to tell from here."

"Damien is inside, isn't he?" Strains of worry sounded in the older woman's voice.

Of course she was worried. This woman had loved Damien for a lifetime.

Addy swallowed hard.

She had only loved him for a few days. She'd nearly told him, just in case. But then stopped herself.

Because what if he didn't feel the same?

She hadn't wanted him distracted from what he needed to do. He'd needed all his wits about him.

Within a matter of moments, the staff had organized, along with several of the male guests, and had begun shuffling buckets of water through the corridors.

The closest source, Addy knew from the recent tour Damien had personally provided, could be accessed in the brewing area itself where water from a nearby spring was piped directly to the large vats.

But had the water been accessible? Nearly an hour had passed since Damien had sent her outside, and in that time, she'd sent up dozens of prayers for his safety.

She couldn't tell for sure if the stinging in her throat and eyes was from the smoke or from holding back tears of apprehension.

The female guests were mostly huddled beneath the pergola behind them, and a handful of older gentlemen looked on from the garden paths.

Most of the younger men had sprung into action. If Addy was going to discover Damien's whereabouts, she was going to have to get closer.

"Stay here. I'll see what I can find out." Addy moved Lady Bloodstone's hand to the railing.

"Oh, thank you, Adelaide." The viscountess nodded.

"I'll stay with Mother." Callie's gaze met Addy's, wide with fear. "Just find Damien."

Addy nodded. This family, unlike many families in the *ton*, loved and relied upon one another.

"Don't do anything reckless," Lady Bloodstone added.

"I won't." Addy backed away and then turned and swiftly made her way back toward the house. As she shuffled past the older gentlemen who'd remained with the women, Addy didn't stop to ask questions, but overheard speculation along the way.

"One of the chimneys failed…"

"Damn reckless to run the operation inside the manor…"

Which confirmed that it was, indeed, the brewing area.

"Addy!" Priscilla caught her arm from behind. "What can I do?"

Addy merely blinked at her at first, but then she was struck with the realization that a houseful of guests was now stranded outside in the middle of the night.

With Lady Bloodstone overwrought, Addy was responsible. "Is there room at Hardwood Cliffhouse? The guests won't be able to sleep here tonight."

Priscilla was already nodding. "Of course. And we'll send for more coaches."

"Priscilla." Addy winced. "Will you watch out for Lady Bloodstone? I need to see... I need to know..."

"Hardwood's gone in as well. But of course!" Lines of worry etched between Priscilla's eyes and in that moment, a knowing passed in that stare between them.

"They'll be fine!" Addy declared it as much for herself as for Priscilla. "They'll be fine."

Priscilla nodded and then the two women separated to go in opposite directions—Addy toward the house and Priscilla toward the stables.

Around the back of the manor, the brigade shuffled buckets of water from a well, along a short path, and into the servants' entrance. Over the clamor of activity and the distant roar of the fire, Addy recognized the butler's voice shouting orders to the servants. "Don't let up, men! We can keep it contained!"

Was Damien on the brigade? But she knew he wouldn't remain outside. He'd be at the front. She cursed. Because, of course, he would be at the front.

She swallowed around the fear that was lodged in her throat.

He was going to be fine.

The fire would be contained.

Careful to keep out of the way, Addy sprinted toward the effort, not caring that the hem of her dress dragged in puddles and mud.

She'd get a quick update and then return to the gazebo to let Lady Bloodstone and Priscilla know what she'd learned.

Please, Damien, be safe!

She couldn't exist in a world without him.

Her heart stopped and the stinging in her throat returned with a vengeance.

"Mr. Pitkins!" She shouted as she neared. He caught her eyes, looking annoyed for an instant, and then waved a hand for her to return to the gardens.

She ignored his command. "Where is the viscount?" She would not go back until she'd learned something.

"You're only in the way here, my lady. Please, go back and wait with the others."

Addy halted. "Do you know Bloodstone's whereabouts? Hardwood's?"

"They'll be fine." He scowled.

Addy turned to the line of workers, noticing that many appeared exhausted while still rapidly handing buckets back and forth between one another.

How could she do nothing while others toiled?

Seeing a gap where one of the younger footmen lagged, Addy ran across and stepped into the line.

"You mustn't—"

"Hand me that." Addy ignored the feeble protest and passed an empty bucket toward the back of the line.

A fire, in the height of summer, threatened to devastate.

All her instincts urged her to go inside and look for Damien, but she'd promised him she'd stay outside. At least if she worked on the brigade, she could do something!

Within minutes, she was soaked and her arms ached, but she welcomed the discomfort in that it provided some distraction from her fear for Damien.

One of the footmen had injured his wrist. As he headed

toward the gazebo, he'd promised to inform Lady Hard-wood of her whereabouts.

Addy could not go back, not with Damien inside. She had learned from those working around her that he had been the one to get the pipes functioning.

Rather than allow herself to dwell on the smoke trapped in those small rooms, or the heat of the flames burning the air he breathed, Addy focused on spilling as little water as possible as she handed off another bucket.

He must be safe.

He must be safe.

She chanted to herself as she moved in tandem with the servants.

In the distance she saw coaches arriving from the nearby village, many to carry guests away to Hardwood Cliffhouse, and some bringing others to assist in the efforts.

The ball had been winding down when the fire broke out, but Addy didn't notice the early morning chill until one of the manservants announced the fire was out and efforts slowed to a halt.

How much time had passed? How long had Damien been inside?

Ignoring her ruined dress, her aching limbs, and all the congratulations going on around her, she scrambled inside, glad she'd had enough time to memorize the twists and turns she'd need to take to get to the tower.

Two right turns here, up a second stairwell. She was grateful that some of the lanterns had been left to light the way through the darkness.

And although the stench of smoke weighted heavily, it lacked the threat of fresh fire. Curtains and rugs would need washing, if not replaced, and wooden surfaces would need scrubbed and polished. But as far as she'd ascertained, no one had been seriously injured. The manor itself remained standing.

But what would she find in the tower?

One more flight of stairs and through a bricked archway, but when Addy turned the last corner to the brewing area, the sight she found stole her breath.

What had once been a gleaming area, outfitted with vats and pipes and tools, now gaped like an open wound. A hole in the floor, and nothing but black where the chimney had stood.

Mr. Rupert, the brewing master Damien had introduced her to the week before, caught sight of her and shook his head. And at first, she thought he was going to order her to leave, but he checked himself.

Perhaps he simply didn't have the energy.

"The north chimney failed. It's a total loss," he said.

Damien's dream.

Thank God her father had provided Damien with her dowry. If not...

Addy didn't allow her thoughts to go there.

"Where is he?" Addy asked.

Mr. Rupert gestured across the room.

A lone figure was bent over with his hands on his knees. Damien glanced up and then back down at the floor without acknowledging her.

Black covered him from head to foot, and he'd have completely disappeared into the charred remains if not for the whites of his eyes.

If ever a man appeared broken, it was this one.

But they had been lucky. Everyone had gotten out safely and most of the manor remained standing.

All was not lost! Ignoring her own exhaustion, Addy picked her way across the room.

"I'm so sorry, Damien." This had been his *dream*.

"You shouldn't be in here." His voice was raw. He didn't rise to stand. He didn't even bother looking up at her.

"No one was badly hurt," she offered. What was there to say?

"My mother—"

"Is fine. She and most of the guests have been taken to Hardwood's estate for the night."

He simply nodded, and Addy crouched down beside him.

"Damien? Are you all right?"

In answer, he shook his head.

"It could have been so much worse." She wanted to reassure him. "Everyone is safe. And aside from damage from the smoke, the main parts of the house are intact."

Still nothing.

"All isn't lost. You have your recipes. I know your father began the brewery in here, but you can make beer anywhere. We can rebuild the brewery, Damien. Perhaps it would be best to build away from the house. You can begin fresh. Have modern pipes installed throughout—"

"With what?" he hissed.

"I know you're upset—and tired. Come out of here with me." He needed fresh air. She moved to take his arm but he shook her off.

"It's over."

Addy flinched. Everything about him felt dark—bleak.

But he'd suffered a great loss tonight.

"It's *not* over."

"Why aren't you at Cliffhouse with the others?" The

question sounded more like an accusation. He swiped his arm across his brow, his cold stare not meeting hers. "What happened to your gown? You said you would stay with my mother."

"She's fine, and so is your sister. I helped with the brigade. I needed to do something, Damien. I couldn't just stand by and watch..." And then almost desperately, "This isn't as bad as it seems. We'll rebuild. It'll be better than it was before—"

But he finally swung his gaze around to meet hers. In his eyes, where she'd always seen light, she only saw darkness.

And anger.

And defeat.

"There is no money, Adelaide." But his words didn't register.

"You have my dowry."

"I don't."

Addy simply shook her head. "What do you mean?" How did a person squander away a hundred thousand pounds? That would be impossible.

"Your father sent a dowry, Adelaide, but it was a pittance —a joke." The laugh that followed his blow was not really a laugh of all.

Addy's breath hitched. "But I thought—"

"I know." Damien was shaking his head, again, avoiding her gaze. "I thought I could keep it from you."

"How much?" A cold weight settled in her heart as not only her future, but the love she'd claimed from the past seemed to drift away. "How much did he send you?"

Damien tilted his head back and stared at the now blackened ceiling. "One hundred pounds, Adelaide. I didn't even bother depositing it."

"So there's no money to rebuild?" This wasn't happening!

"No, Adelaide." He tightened his mouth. "There's nothing." And then he stared down at the floor again. "And now no brewery, either."

LEGACY IN JEOPARDY

Blood roared in Addy's ears as the meaning of his words settled in.

One hundred pounds?

How could her father do that to her? She'd been wrong about him after all. Rather than ensure she found happiness, it seemed he'd preferred to make a mockery of England's most noble of gentlemen.

At her expense.

Because he didn't care. Her father didn't care about her. Had he ever?

Addy moved listlessly as Damien turned her to exit toward their chambers.

She stared straight ahead, moving woodenly. How did her feet keep moving when her world had just collapsed?

This time was so much worse than before.

She'd never *loved* Marcus.

"Why didn't you tell me the truth?" she asked.

"I—" he shook his head rather than provide an explanation.

Addy cleared her throat—from the effects of the smoke the night before, or from an abundance of emotion? "You led me to believe it was enough." Which in turn had made her believe that *she* had been enough. "Why would you do that? Why did you lie to me?"

"It was for your own good. Let's not get into this now." His voice came out hoarse, followed by a fit of coughing. How much smoke had he inhaled throughout the night?

They arrived at the entrance to her half of their chambers, but rather then enter alongside her, he opened it and released her arm.

"You aren't coming in...?" He must be as exhausted as she was. He needed water. He needed to rest. He needed...

Her dowry.

"I don't have time now. I'm sure the bishop's heard about the fire, but I'll send word over that we need to postpone the ceremony."

Their *wedding ceremony...*

The ceremony which Addy had agreed to believing her dowry would be sufficient to cover estate and brewery costs.

Damien was correct in assuming that they couldn't possibly have their ceremony that morning, but was he correct to assume there would be any ceremony at all?

Because this changed everything!

Addy halted in the threshold, wanting to say something but not knowing what. "Don't you want to—"

But he cut her off. "This isn't the time. I need to get this estate functioning again. Get out of that damp gown, Addy. Get some sleep. We'll talk about this later."

Of course.

He was Bloodstone. If he failed, his legacy died.

Responsibilities didn't stop merely because he'd been up all night fighting a fire.

Addy stared up at him, searching his gaze for the reassurance he'd always had for her.

For an instant, she thought she saw a glimmer, but then it was gone.

Guilt shot through her. Believing he had her dowry, Addy thought he had options.

His mother could lose her home. His sister's future would be jeopardized.

And all the tenants, and servants... What of their livelihoods?

Marrying her would be the biggest mistake of his life. Yes, the fire had been devastating, but ultimately the loss of her dowry was the real tragedy.

She should have realized it had been too good to be true.

Loving him—believing she deserved to be loved back, that she belonged, had been a foolish dream. A shudder ran through her.

She could not go through with it.

Addy memorized the face of the person who owned her heart.

But she saw beyond his looks, she knew his thoughts beyond his charm, she knew the power in his heart, not only his title.

He cared for her, yes, and he'd wanted to do the honorable thing where she was concerned.

But ultimately, other, much greater burdens weighed him down.

"I'll clean up." And then she would climb into the bed she'd shared with him every night since arriving. Would he join her?

Her arms ached to hold him, to soothe the tension from his shoulders and back. She wanted to absorb his defeat, to return all the comfort he'd ever given her.

She couldn't bring herself to end it yet.

"Don't be long," she said instead, watching him hopefully.

The hint of affection she yearned to see in his expression never appeared. "Get some sleep, Addy."

He was not coming to her tonight. Perhaps the choice wasn't hers to make.

Their ardor for one another had been powerful, but in the wake of disappointment and loss, that would never be enough.

"Good night, Damien," she said.

But he was gone.

He'd already left.

***

Damien hadn't meant to tell her like that. Hell, he hadn't wanted to tell her at all. But on the heels of the worst night of his life, she'd stood beside him with a sickeningly hopeful smile as though his future hadn't just gone up in smoke.

Literally and figuratively.

Even if he hadn't told her, she'd have discovered the truth soon enough.

When he couldn't afford to rebuild—or keep the estate fully staffed—or pay off the tradesmen who provided daily goods.

She'd expected him to go to bed with her, but he could not.

Dragging his hand along the banister, he grimaced at the

line his fingertips made in the thin layer of soot. One night. It had only taken one night to change the course of his life forever.

Hell, to change the course of his legacy.

And it was his fault. He'd known the chimney needed repair and had put it off. His nose and throat burned from the smoke, but not nearly as much as his chest burned at the knowledge that this could have been prevented.

He'd been wrong to believe he didn't need to marry well—wrong to assume he could have Adelaide. He'd been arrogant to imagine he could do what other titled gentlemen could not—marry for love rather than necessity.

And it stung.

More than that, it was like a dagger to the chest.

Because he'd made her promises. His mind flashed images of her tossing that damn bouquet, plucking a truffle off his plate, laughing with his mother.

And how she'd looked just before the ball. She'd been filled with confidence and hope—as beautiful as he'd ever seen her.

Just now, she'd wanted him in her bed. She'd wanted...

Him.

Other memories, sensations as much as images, slowed his steps—memories of her beneath him, of being inside her, of her fingers digging into his back...

He'd make love to her. There was always time to make love with that woman. She'd understand why he'd lied to her. Words wouldn't be necessary.

But she...

Was.

And then he'd face this mess.

Urgency had him turning to go back to her chamber at the same moment Pitkins appeared on the landing.

The man had worked tirelessly, heading up the brigade and ensuring the main part of the house was protected. And yet somehow he stood at attention, looking as unruffled as he had the day before.

Damien's throat thickened. "My thanks for all your efforts." He gave the man a meaningful nod.

"Simply protecting our home," the butler answered.

Damien nodded. Pitkins was correct. Reddington Park was home to more than just himself, his mother, and Caledonia.

And Adelaide.

His precious Adelaide.

She hadn't deserved his foul mood. He'd heard the words coming from his mouth, knowing she didn't deserve them, and yet he'd done nothing to stop them.

Because none of this was her fault, and yet he'd not be in this predicament if not for her.

She'd come into his life and disrupted all his carefully laid plans.

But that wasn't fair.

He was as much to blame as anyone. And his life wasn't the only one that had been disrupted.

He imagined how events might have ordered themselves if he had not insisted on escorting her home following Edgeworth's wedding.

There would have been no article in the Gazette. No shared night in that rundown inn.

No kisses in the carriage.

No conversations peppered with odd tidbits of information. No hair tickling his chin at night.

Not to mention all the other depraved intimacies he'd come to crave.

He'd left her looking exhausted as he was. Likely she'd fallen asleep the moment her head hit the pillow.

An empty darkness opened inside him.

"My lord?" Mr. Pitkins had been talking to him. "The servants are beginning the clean-up."

Damien shook off his melancholy. His 'apology' would have to wait.

"That's fine. But bring in a physician to ensure there weren't any unreported injuries. And have them work in short shifts. Now's not the time to overwork the staff."

"Right, my lord."

Damien nodded. "I'll meet with Hardwood, but I'm certain he'll be happy to house my mother and Caledonia, and any other guests who aren't prepared to end their visits early."

"And what of the viscountess, my lord?"

"She's at Hardwood Cliffhouse already."

"Not the dowager, my lord. Your wife. I begged her to go back with the other guests but she refused. She worked beside the heartiest of the men, not once stopping to rest. If she hadn't already earned the staff's respect, she won the last one over last night. Shall I send the physician to her chamber first?"

That was why her gown had been soaked.

Damien closed his eyes. He was a heel, thinking only of himself when she'd found him in the tower.

He'd promised to take care of her, and yet how many times had he already failed?

"She's currently resting, but when the servants return,

send her maid... Diana, is it? Tell her not to wake the viscountess, though, if she's still sleeping."

It was important Damien thank all of the servants for stepping up. Especially those who'd put their lives on the line.

Which meant he needed to put off the inexplicable need he felt to go to Adelaide until later.

After he'd tended to his duties. After he'd sent word to the bishop.

He ran a hand through his hair, disgusted when it came away with flecks of ash and soot.

And, of course, he couldn't go to her until after he'd had a bath.

Taking care of these matters first, however, allowed him time to formulate his explanation for lying to her. And to imagine all the ways he would make his apology.

And then tomorrow, they'd drive to the church two villages away and make their marriage official.

He'd made promises, not only to Adelaide but to Miss Primm. He'd shared a suite with her here, but also at Longbow Castle. He'd even returned the signed contracts to her father.

Hell, he'd been sharing her bed for weeks.

Dowry or not, Damien was going to make Adelaide Royal his wife.

And despite everything else, that thought was the one that got him through the day.

With Adelaide at his side, they'd find a way to rebuild.

She'd turned his life upside down but—he smiled for the first time that morning—perhaps it was what he'd needed all along.

With a new surge of energy, Damien tended to all the

tasks he'd made for himself, and several he'd not. It was late in the afternoon before he returned for a well-needed bath, followed by a shave, which together made him feel half-human once again.

He'd ordered dinner sent up to Adelaide's chamber while he dressed, and by the time his valet tied off his cravat, he was fairly certain she'd be well-rested.

He'd hold her in his arms tonight. He'd belatedly provide the comfort she'd sought from him earlier.

And when he finally stepped into the adjoining chamber, he was eager to make his apologies—eager to move forward with his wife.

It was not Adelaide who greeted him, however, but her maid.

"Is she still sleeping?" He'd not be deterred, he'd simply join her beneath the coverlet.

His palms itched as he imagined stirring her to wakefulness. He'd not only use his hands, but also his mouth. He'd whisper how precious she was to him and then taste her everywhere.

"Is she not with you, my lord?" the maid interrupted his less-than-proper thoughts.

"She was here when I left." Damien strode from the sitting room into her bedchamber. "Adelaide?"

But she was not tucked beneath the covers. The coverlet was wrinkled, as though it had been pulled back, but it didn't look to have been slept in.

Where the devil was she?

The hair on the back of Damien's neck pricked up, and he marched back to where Diana stood wringing her hands.

"Was she here when you arrived?" he forcibly kept himself from demanding.

The maid shook her head.

Perplexed, Damien glanced around the room. Had she decided to move to Hardwood's estate as well? Wouldn't the earl have mentioned that?

The maid opened a door to one of the dressing rooms, as though looking for Addy in one of them. "Ah, but her small valise is gone. She must have gone to Cliffhouse after all."

He and Hardwood had touched on the necessity of moving back the wedding ceremony, but then they'd also discussed the extent of the damages from the fire, and some possibilities for rebuilding the brewery.

It was possible Addy's arrival had slipped the earl's mind altogether.

It was also possible he hadn't even known she was there.

Lady Hardwood was a good friend to Addy. Damien had left her upset. He'd been horrid to her.

Of course, she'd have wanted to go to her friend.

It was the only possibility that made sense.

ONCE AND FOR ALL

delaide dropped her gaze from the passing scenery to the paper she'd taken from Damien's desk. The handwriting was scrawled—nearly impossible to make out.

Unless, of course, one had been reading it since they were a child.

Damien had left her alone, insisting she rest, but—even after changing out of the damp gown, washing up, donning her night rail, and climbing under the coverlet—sleep had eluded her. She'd tried reading, but even Holden Hampden's stories were yet another reminder of Damien.

No matter that she was physically exhausted, her mind wouldn't allow her peace until she could parse out all that had happened in the past twelve hours.

Frustrated, she'd leapt off the bed, changed into one of her day gowns, and meandered the halls until she'd found herself in Damien's study.

It had been empty, almost as though he was avoiding her. Rather than walk in circles again, however, she'd decided to wait for him.

She'd only ventured inside a few times since arriving at Reddington Park, so instead of making herself comfortable on the leather settee, she took a turn about the room. Moving around the perimeter, she'd examined bookshelves, artifacts, and took note of the spirits he kept in a liquor cabinet.

The door was snug, which was lucky, as it had mostly protected the furnishings from the acrid smoke. Addy had removed a book and inhaled the leathery scent. She'd also caught a hint of lemon oil and bergamot.

It had reminded her of Damien.

Was everything to remind her of Damien?

Growing bolder in her explorations, she'd edged around the large mahogany desk and lowered herself into the well-worn chair. How many viscounts had sat right here? She'd imagined Damien struggling to go through reports and documents while sitting at his father's desk.

He did not take his duties lightly. She'd hoped she could be a helpmate.

For no reason other than idle curiosity, she'd opened the top drawer. And there, she'd discovered her father's address and the special license—nearly identical to the one she and Damien had signed as witnesses less than one month ago.

This time, their two names were on the lines for bride and groom.

The mail coach hit a rut, jolting Addy back to the present, and she stared out at a countryside that was becoming all-too familiar to her.

She'd been gone for a little over four hours now.

Had he discovered her absence yet, or was he still rushing around the estate, overseeing the beginnings of the cleaning and repairs?

She'd removed the two documents from the drawer and sat them side by side on the desk. On her right, the license; on her left, her father's whereabouts.

And on the corner of the desk, a pile of what appeared to be unpaid bills.

Damn her father for doing something so cruel!

From the second Damien had disclosed the amount her father had sent, Addy had been confused and then hurt.

And then lost.

But whether it was by accident or fate, staring at those papers, her path became perfectly clear.

If she gave into her heart and married Damien without facing her father, she would forever be in his life, but so would those bills. How long before her husband resented her?

She needed answers. A good portion of her dowry had been earned by her father, that was true, but the first of it had been bequeathed to her by her mother.

He'd had no right to keep it to himself, and yet Addy had never confronted him.

She would find him now. She'd demand answers, but also demand what was hers.

She would take him to task for the cavalier decisions he'd made without considering her future—or her feelings.

Sending such a paltry amount had been a slap in the face —a blatant insult—not only to the man who'd wanted to marry her—but to her.

His daughter. His flesh and blood.

Logically, she knew the amount didn't reflect her value as a human being, but…

It hurt.

With her decision made, Addy had packed a single valise,

hitched a ride into the village, and purchased the last ticket available to ride the next mail coach to London.

Public transportation, she noted, was vastly inferior to the luxury of Primm's coach.

She squirmed and stuffed the paper with her father's address back into her reticule.

And for the first time in over thirty-six hours, Addy closed her eyes, gave into the jostling and the rocking, and finally slept.

***

A little over twenty-four hours later, Addy was once again in Mayfair.

And, fearful that she'd lose her courage, she'd not bothered going to Victoria's townhouse to sleep, or to wash up and change.

She went directly to her father's address.

And now that she was here, nerves shot through her veins as she matched the number on the house to the one on the paper.

Ironically, it was only a few houses down from Damien's.

Damien. Her dear lion.

She pinched her mouth together to keep it from trembling.

Part of her felt guilty that she hadn't said goodbye—that she hadn't told him she was leaving and what she planned to do.

But he would have insisted they go through with the ceremony first. And for as long as she'd known him, he'd been impossible for her to resist.

So she'd left him to deal with the aftermath of the fire alone.

Would he miss her?

She missed him more than she could possibly have imagined.

She wouldn't dwell on the fact that she might not ever see him again. She needed to be strong for this meeting, and arriving to confront her father while a heartbroken mess likely wouldn't help her.

If the address proved to be incorrect, or if her father had left the country again, Addy would resort to the new backup plan that she'd devised.

At least that was what she told herself.

Regardless, she would not return to Reddington Park emptyhanded. She would not be the burden that sunk the ship.

If he truly required a huge amount of funds to shore up his family's legacy, and if she could not provide that for him, then she'd leave him free to find some lady who had a proper dowry.

And Addy, well. She would take temporary refuge at Victoria's townhouse, empty out her savings, and buy passage on a ship back to America.

It was an ambitious and slightly terrifying plan, but in the wake of the very public ball Lady Bloodstone had thrown to celebrate a marriage that had never taken place, her and Damien's deception would eventually get out. His reputation, she surmised, would recover. He was a viscount and he was a man.

Adelaide's reputation, on the other hand, would never recover from such a scandal—if she was left with one at all.

No one would employ her, and Addy knew her aunt well enough to know she'd not find refuge there.

Addy would well and truly be on her own.

If she returned to America, however, she could leave her reputation behind. And with an ocean between her and the man who owned her heart, she stood a chance at dismantling the hopes and dreams she'd built around him.

He was not her husband yet, and if she failed to bring her father around today, he never would be.

She swallowed the swell of emotion in her throat and pounded the knocker three times.

WHERE IS ADELAIDE?

*I*t had only taken one day to air out the main rooms in the manor, and so early the next morning, Damien sent the carriage over to Cliffhouse to convey Adelaide, his mother, and Caledonia back to Reddington park.

Warmth shot through his veins, a combination of nervousness and anticipation.

He'd missed Adelaide. He hadn't expected that.

He'd apologize for misleading her. She would forgive him, because she would understand, and because she was Adelaide.

He would not wait until evening to have her alone.

"Lady Hardwood is a most welcoming hostess." His mother's face was the first to appear from inside the carriage as she ducked through the opening and allowed Damien to assist her to solid ground. "I'm happy to be home, though. I know you said the damages were limited to the tower but I'll feel better to see for myself."

With her head tilted back and her eyes focused on nothing in particular, she smiled at her words.

"It's good to have you home, Mother," Damien said as his mother's companion exited the coach without assistance.

"I can't imagine the damage is significant if you allowed Adelaide to remain."

Damien had just been turning to the coach again when his mother's words halted him.

"But she was at Cliffhouse." Damien leaned into the vehicle, fully expecting to meet Addy's wide green stare, and couldn't contain his disappointment to only find one similar to his own.

Callie.

"Is Adelaide coming in a separate carriage?" he asked. But he wondered if perhaps she'd been so angry with him that she wasn't yet prepared to come home.

The realization irritated him, but he supposed he deserved it. He'd been cold and distant with her after the fire.

He'd not been himself.

"But she stayed here. She stayed behind." Callie frowned. "Damien, Adelaide was not at Cliffhouse."

What? No, that was impossible. If she was not at Cliffhouse, then...

"Are you certain?"

"Quite."

His mother frowned at the turn of conversation. "It was remarked upon more than once. By Lady Hardwood and by her sisters. Even a few of the servants congratulated me on having a daughter-in-law who would work alongside the men in fighting the fire. And they applauded her dedication to you, in that she'd chosen to remain with her new husband rather than retire to safer lodgings. She is here, Damien."

But she was not. The hair that had pricked up on the back of his neck the day before now stood at full attention.

"Hardwood's mother found it most fortuitous that you'd found a lady who wasn't only intelligent, but also well-dowered."

Damien ran a hand through his hair. His mother was living under so many untruths that he didn't know where to begin.

But most pressing of all, he needed to ascertain Adelaide's whereabouts.

Tamping down his panic, he turned toward the open door and hailed Mr. Pitkins. "Lady Bloodstone is missing." He wouldn't waste time with further explanation. "I want a search organized right away. Inside the house, as well as the grounds."

It was possible she'd injured herself inspecting some damaged part of the house. It was also possible that she'd fallen ill from having breathed in too much smoke from the fire, or taken a chill from all but dousing herself while she'd toiled in the brigade.

Thunder roared in his ears as he fought to maintain his calm.

He pictured her gown, sopping wet, and how her dampened hair had escaped her coiffure to trail around her face and down her back.

He'd walked away from her, unwilling to discuss his lie —unwilling to explain their dire circumstances.

But then he remembered her maid mentioning that Adelaide's valise was missing.

This time, rather than run his hand through his hair, Damien grasped a handful and tugged on it painfully.

Where had she gone? Surely not the school. She could be anywhere.

"I don't understand, Damien. What can have happened to her?"

He took hold of his mother's hand and squeezed it.

He froze inside. This was his fault.

"She's left me." The instant the words left his mouth he knew they must be true.

"But I don't understand, why would she do that?"

Damien would still have the estate searched, but he knew Adelaide wouldn't be found.

He leaned closer to his mother so as not to broadcast his next statement to all asunder. And then lowering his voice, he said, "There was no marriage, Mother. And there is no dowry."

His mother, forever graceful under all circumstances, nodded slowly.

His knees, however, had weakened and his heart seemed to have lodged itself in the back of his throat. He could live without a brewery. He could live with his manor falling apart around him.

The earth shifted beneath his feet.

Because the one thing he couldn't live without, the one person in the world he could not live without...

Was, no doubt, somewhere on the road to London.

"Come inside, Damien." His mother had turned toward the house.

"I need to go—"

"Yes, you must go after her. But Adelaide's no fool, and if

she left, she had good reason. Before you take to the road yet again, lets discuss what you're going to tell her when you catch up with her."

A MISUNDERSTANDING

"*I* am so pleased to finally meet you." A smart-looking woman with blond and silver hair crossed to meet Addy at the door before the butler could formally announce her.

Addy frowned, confused until she caught sight of her father, who'd risen from the settee but seemed to hold himself back.

Which was unusual, as uncertainty was the one thing she'd never witnessed in the man who'd raised her. He looked older, which she had expected, his hair more white than brown, and he'd put on a few pounds. But she also spied something she had not expected.

Despite the hint of hesitation in his eyes, he looked...

Happy?

Addy straightened her back, summoning the outrage she'd carried throughout most of her journey.

"I'm afraid I don't have the luxury of knowing anything about you." Addy kept her voice steady.

The woman was all smiles and eager welcome. It would

be easy to act thusly, Addy supposed, when one's husband had not been mocked for marrying her.

Addy's father stepped forward, and for a moment she thought he was going to take her hands, or even embrace her.

Nine years had passed since they'd seen one another. Although they'd not been outwardly affectionate since she'd been a child, she'd imagined some sign after all this time.

But instead, he put one hand on the other woman's back. "Addy, may I present you to my wife. Estelle, as you've guessed, this is my daughter, Adelaide."

As shocking as it was to hear that her father had married, she was nearly as startled that he'd perform proper introductions.

But...

Wife?

"When?" she asked. "This seems like the sort of news a father might share with his daughter." Her umbrage had returned in full. She swallowed hard, past the hurt and betrayal to which she ought to be immune by now.

"Recently," he turned to smile at the woman beside him —at his wife! And in that look, he sent affection she'd half-hoped to see directed at herself.

"We met at the end of the season when your father saved my favorite bonnet from sinking in the Thames. We've only been married for two weeks now."

The woman, who was staring at Addy's father as though he'd hung the moon, was British and very proper. A widow, perhaps?

Addy inhaled. "How... romantic."

She didn't know quite what to say. Two weeks? Only a

little longer than she'd been married to Damien—since she'd *reportedly* been married to Damien, that was.

"And you are newlywed as well." Estelle, nay, *Mrs. Royal*, peered around Addy as though looking for someone. "Are you and the viscount in London on holiday?"

"My daughter, a bloody viscountess." Her father spoke with pride, and Addy fisted her hands at her side. How dare he? "Estelle is a lady as well," he went on. "A duchess."

"My late husband was the Duke of Crawford." A shadow flickered across her expression. "But I am quite happy to concede the title to my daughter-in-law. I'm even happier to be Mrs. Royal."

Addy did not want to like this woman who'd usurped her mother's place, but Estelle's pleasant nature made it almost impossible not to.

But wait—her father was married to a *duchess?*

All of this felt like a puzzle—a puzzle with missing pieces. She glanced around the room. It looked lived in.

Cozy.

Paintings hung on the walls, which were covered in a burgundy and gold damask. The furnishings were elegant, but a little worn, as were the rich carpets beneath them.

This was not only a house. It was a home.

Several papers were strewn on the small table that sat in front of the settee, peppered with her father's handwriting.

She stood silent for so long that both her father and his new wife stilled, studying her with...

Concern?

"Is Lord Bloodstone not with you?" her father asked. "If he's not treating you properly, by God—"

"You'll what, father, take back your hundred pounds?" Addy couldn't contain herself a second longer.

"What the devil are you talking about?" He scowled. This was the father she knew, grousing and demanding.

That was, until his wife turned and set her hand on his shoulder. "Charles."

That was all it took.

Her look and the touch of her hand.

"Forgive me, Estelle, Adelaide." The color in his cheeks subsided, but he wasn't finished. He returned to his place on the settee, and his new wife took the spot beside him.

"Where is Lord Bloodstone, Addy," he asked. "And what do you mean, one hundred pounds?"

Her father's wife looked to Addy with equal curiosity.

Addy blinked. "That's the amount you sent." But her father was shaking his head.

As was Estelle.

"He sent one hundred thousand pounds, my dear."

"Estelle wouldn't marry me otherwise. When we came across that announcement, she insisted I do right by you."

"That was horrid, what he did to you all those years ago," Estelle added. The sympathy on her face was real.

Addy stared at where her father's hand clutched his wife. Estelle turned to him with raised eyebrows, as though she were prompting an unruly child.

"Estelle made me see the only person I'd hurt was you." Her father looked sheepish. "Can you forgive me?"

But... If her father had sent one hundred thousand pounds...

Addy's gaze shot to the papers with her father's handwriting.

Barely legible.

Her heart skipped a beat. Was it possible Damien had read the numbers incorrectly?

"I think…" Addy's voice caught. "I think there's been a terrible mistake."

"Where is the viscount, Addy?" her father asked.

But even before she could answer, a commotion at the door had them all swinging their stares toward the foyer.

The sight there sent her heart racing.

Dusty from the road and flushed from exertion, Damien pushed past the butler to hover in the threshold.

Like a lion. *Her lion.*

And when his gaze locked with hers, the pain she saw in those beautiful eyes sent guilt shooting through her.

"Adelaide," he said her name with as much relief as hurt. All that they'd been through, and then she'd left without a word.

She should have told him she was leaving.

She required all her self-control to keep from bursting into tears.

"You left," he added.

She wanted to throw herself into his arms and give in to the tears stinging the backs of her eyes, but she needed to know why he had come.

Because—even if she now felt much more optimistic about their situation—she, too, was hurt.

If Estelle hadn't risen and crossed to welcome him, Addy had no idea how long the two of them would have stood staring at one another as the tension in the room crescendoed.

"My lord. We were just asking her ladyship if you were in town." Her father's new wife beckoned to their butler. "Mr. Martin, will you have tea brought in for us, please?"

Tea, Addy conceded, sounded wonderful.

"Bloodstone." Addy's father's tone hung in the air like an accusation.

She needed to clear the air about her dowry, but before she could formulate how to go about doing that, Damien was across the room, taking her hands in his.

"Adelaide." His eyes pleaded with hers. "Forgive me?"

"Of course—" She reached up to touch his cheek. She'd only just arrived in London that morning. Had he ridden through the night to catch up to her?

"I should have told you everything rather than leave you alone after the fire—I should have told you the truth before then. But—" his gaze narrowed as he shot a scowl across the room to her father before bringing it back to hers—"you were just so damn happy."

"I know. Oh, Damien. The dowry—"

"Doesn't matter." His throat moved, and then he did the last thing she'd ever expected.

With her hands still clasped in his, he dropped to one knee. "You're all that matters. *You.* God, when I realized you'd left, I could barely breathe. I don't need a dowry. Hell, I don't even need the brewery. All I need is you."

"But—"

"Because when I'm with you. When I have you at my side, I can do anything. You energize me. You make everything in my life brighter—more colorful." He tilted his head, and his eyes shone a little more than normal. "I love you more than life itself. Marry me, Adelaide?" He reached into his jacket, his gaze pinned to hers.

As though his future hung on her answer.

As though this was the most important moment in his life.

"Make me the happiest of men, Adelaide?" The license was identical to the one she'd torn up.

"What the hell is going on?" her father demanded, but Addy ignored him.

"You love me?" Addy froze, mesmerized by his declaration.

Damien loved her!

"With all my heart." A lock of his golden hair had fallen along his face, but he didn't seem to notice.

She reached across and pushed it away.

He had never looked so earnest. "Please?" His voice caught.

"Yes!" Addy had nothing to keep her from throwing herself into his arms, nearly knocking him backward in the process.

"Are the two of you not already married?" Estelle's question reminded Addy that they weren't alone.

But she didn't care! Damien wanted to marry her regardless of her dowry—and not because he had to—because he wanted to!

Because she brought color into his life.

She rubbed her face into his chest, wiping away happy tears. She needed to gather her composure and clear matters up with her father.

She felt Damien's lips on her head, and then her shoulder. "Thank God," he murmured. "I thought you were going to be stubborn and fight me on this."

She leaned back, holding his gaze cautiously. "About the dowry..."

"It's all right. We'll figure it out."

She shook her head. "I think there's been a misunderstanding."

At this, Damien seemed to decide they had a few details to clear up. Keeping one arm around her, he drew both of them up to face her father.

"Pardon me sir," he stiffened beside Addy. "But you have a hell of a way of caring for your daughter."

VOWS

*D*amien's tone and Addy's father's clenched fists had Addy worried that one of them was going to attack the other.

"Wait, Damien." She would not release his arm. The woman who was her stepmother now was doing the same with her father.

For an instant, she locked eyes with the former duchess, startled in an ironic way that the two of them had anything in common.

Damien removed his stare from her father just long enough to glance down at Addy.

"Perhaps your father and I should handle this in private."

"No!" Addy and Estelle both answered at the same time. Left alone, there was no telling what these two men might do to one another.

"Damien," Addy demanded his attention. "Do you still have the note?"

"I burned the bloody thing." He turned back to her father. "You exposed your daughter to ridicule out of meaningless pride. And if abandoning her wasn't enough, you mock her by sending that so-called dowry."

Addy winced but had to stop him. "He didn't send one *hundred* pounds. *Damien.* He sent one hundred *thousand* pounds." She dragged her teeth across her bottom lip. "The ink on the parchment must have bled... And my father's handwriting really is atrocious."

She knew the moment he realized what she was saying. His mouth dropped open. His muscles turned to steel beneath her hands.

The last thing in the world she wanted to do was embarrass him.

Her father rubbed his chin and his outrage seemed to have dissipated. "You burnt a note for one hundred thousand pounds?" And then he glanced between the two of them. "But you signed the contracts anyway."

Damien exhaled. "No amount of money is worth more than Adelaide. She's the true prize." He ran a shaking hand through his hair, breaking the tension in the air with a self-deprecating laugh.

His words, however, seared themselves onto her soul. *No amount of money was worth more than her? She was the true prize?*

If she hadn't already teared up, she would have done so now.

And then Damien exhaled and turned, pressing the license into Addy's hands. "I think you'd best read this, love. Make sure it's correct before we take it to the church."

Love.

Her heart overflowed as she took the document out of his hands. She loved him so very, very much. "When do you want to go?" she asked.

He bent down to press his mouth to hers and, when he ended the kiss, squeezed her hands.

"Is now too soon?"

They'd waited too long already. Adelaide laughed and then swiped at an errant tear. "Not at all." And then she turned to her father and his new wife.

"Would the two of you like to witness our wedding?"

***

Later that same day, Damien stood at the altar in the same church where they'd witnessed Edgeworth and his bride's nuptials a month prior.

Adelaide stood at his side.

The flowers had been purchased at the last minute by her stepmother, and her father had walked her down the center aisle to meet him and now stood on Damien's opposite side as witness.

It was not at all the ceremony he'd imagined, but at this point, all he cared about was securing Adelaide as his wife.

And this time, when he whisked her away from the church, he'd be taking her to his townhouse—to his chamber, and he didn't give a rat's ass what was written in the Gazette about them.

"I, Adelaide Elizabeth Royal, take you, Damien Thaddeus Reddington, to be my husband." Her voice came out quiet but sure. "To have and to hold from this day forward, in sickness and in health, to love and to cherish, until we are parted by death."

Damien exhaled tension he hadn't realized he'd been holding. No woman had ever commanded his everything like this one had—almost from the moment he'd met her.

He should have known that she was his other half. That she was the person to match up with his soul.

"Do you have a ring, my lord?" The bishop addressed him. Adelaide shook her head but Damien reached into his pocket.

The bloodstone, a smooth black oval containing flecks of scarlet, had been set in intricately woven black gold. Both their hands shook a little as he slid it on her ring finger.

Adelaide blinked and lifted her gaze to meet his.

"My mother wanted you to have it," he answered the question in her eyes. It wasn't the most valuable stone, by any means, but it had been in his family for generations.

"She knows?"

Damien nodded. "It was her idea." He lifted her hand to his mouth. "She and Callie love you. You're already a part of our family."

She made a small choking sound. "I'm glad. I'm so glad she knows the truth."

The bishop spoke a prayer over the ring, and when Damien slipped it onto her finger, it fit as though made for her.

"I give you this ring as a symbol of my vow," Damien's throat thickened. "And with all that I am, and all that I have. I honor you."

Her hands felt frail in his, but these hands were anything but.

As was this woman.

"Those whom God has joined together, let no one put asunder." The bishop's final words echoed off the stone in the empty sanctuary. "You may kiss your bride."

It was the moment he'd waited for all day.

Damien gathered her in his arms and poured as much of himself into the kiss as he dared.

And when they walked out into the sunshine after the ceremony, he leaned down and whispered.

"Do you think this bouquet will bring good luck?" He asked the same question they'd pondered earlier that summer.

"I don't need luck," she smiled up at him. And then she added... "I have you."

—The End—

BEATRICE WOLCOTT and The Marquess of Sexton's story is next, in **Make Believe with the Marquess.**

Beatrice Wolcott is desperate to keep her past a secret. She can't afford to make the same mistake other teachers have made—mistakes that have forced them to marry! So when the Marquess asks Beatrice to pose as his temporary fiancée, she would have refused... Until he offered to discover the identity of whoever has been vandalizing the school. How could she not agree to the bargain when the safety of the students is at stake? **Make Believe with the Marquess.**

MISS PRIMM'S SECRET SCHOOL FOR
BUDDING BLUESTOCKINGS

A NEW ANNABELLE ANDERS SERIES

TRAPPED WITH THE DUKE

Miss Colette Jones

EDUCATED BY THE EARL

Miss Victoria Shipley

PRETENDING TO BE A DEBUTANTE

Lady Priscilla

RESCUED BY THE RAKE

Miss Chloe Fortune

ADVISING THE VISCOUNT

Miss Addy

MAKE BELIEVE WITH THE MARQUESS

Miss Beatrice Wolcott

SCHOOLED BY THE BASTARD

Miss Primm

January 2023

ABOUT THE AUTHOR

Married to the same man for over 25 years, I am a mother to three children and two Miniature Wiener dogs.

After owning a business and experiencing considerable success, my husband and I got caught in the financial crisis and lost everything in 2008; our business, our home, even our car.

At this point, I put my B.A. in Poly Sci to use and took work as a waitress and bartender (Insert irony). Unwilling to give up on a professional life, I simultaneously went back to college and obtained a degree in EnergyManagement.

And then the energy market dropped off.

And then my dog died.

I can only be grateful for this series of unfortunate events, for, with nothing to lose and completely demoralized, I sat down and began to write the romance novels which had until then, existed only my imagination. After publishing over twenty novels now, with one having been nominated for RWA's Distinguished ™RITA Award in 2019, I am happy to tell you that I have finally found my place in life.

Thank you so much for being a part of my journey!

To find out more about my books, and also to download a free novella, get all the info at my website!

www.annabelleanders.com

Made in the USA
Columbia, SC
06 October 2022

68955344R00178